THE MOVIE NOVEL

BY LOUISE GIKOW

SCHOLASTIC INC.

NEW YORK   TORONTO   LONDON   AUCKLAND   SYDNEY

MEXICO CITY   NEW DELHI   HONG KONG   BUENOS AIRES

No part of this work may be reproduced in whole or in part, stored in a retrieval system, or transmitted in any form or by any means, electronic, mechanical, photocopying, recording, or otherwise, without written permission of the publisher. For information regarding permission, write to Scholastic Inc., Attention: Permissions Department, 557 Broadway, New York, NY 10012

ISBN: 0-439-80141-9

Published by Scholastic Inc.
SCHOLASTIC and associated logos are trademarks and/or registered trademarks of Scholastic Inc.

12 11 10 9 8 7 6 5 4 3 2 1   6 7 8 9 10/0

Printed in the U.S.A.
First printing, May 2006
Designed by Rick DeMonico

ONE

Clink! Clink! Clink! Clink!

RJ Raccoon dropped three quarters and a dime into the big silver vending machine. His nose twitched, and he licked his lips. He sighed, and a cloud of vapor formed in the chilly evening air.

Potato chips, he thought. *My favorite food. Now, come to papa . . . !*

He pushed the bright red button, and a trapdoor opened beneath the chips bag. The bag stuck before falling.

RJ stared at the vending machine in disbelief.

Oh, no! My chips!

RJ frowned. He wanted those chips. He needed those chips. He just had to have their crunchy, salty goodness!

But what could he do?

He thought for a second. Then he backed up about ten feet, got off to a running start and rammed into the machine.

Crash!

The machine rocked a little. Inside, the potato chip bag shook slightly. But it stayed firmly lodged where it was.

RJ reached into the old golf bag where he kept all his stuff. He pulled out a shark head grabber arm and stuck it up into the machine. He fished around for a minute, trying to grab the potato chip bag and drag it out.

No dice.

He whacked the arm against the vending machine. The arm cracked into three pieces.

RJ pulled a boomerang out of his bag — retrieved from a Dumpster outside a toy store — and threw it at the machine.

The boomerang hit the machine hard and dropped to the ground. The machine didn't even move.

In a fury, RJ grabbed a golf club out of the bag and hammered at the vending machine's glass front.

Get . . . out . . . of . . . there! he shrieked silently.

Nada.

He glared at the vending machine. It stood there impassively.

RJ's tummy rumbled. He had to have some chips. *Now.* But how was he going to get them?

He stood for a moment, gazing mournfully into the machine's glass panel.

Reflected in it was a cliff. And at the top of that cliff . . .

RJ stared.

Vincent, he thought.

He shook his head. *Bad idea,* he warned himself.

His tummy rumbled again, and he burped.

But sometimes, he realized, *bad ideas were all you had.*

With a flick of his furry tail, he turned, raced across the rest-stop parking lot, and vanished into the woods.

About a half a mile away, RJ stopped at the base of the cliff.

In a cave at the top of the cliff lived Vincent. Vincent was a huge grizzly bear with smelly breath and a bad attitude. He was a bear who always stored away lots of food for when he woke up after the long, cold winter — a bear who wouldn't care if a hungry raccoon borrowed just a little of that food.

Well, anyway, a bear who was hibernating, so he wouldn't know a thing about it.

RJ reached into his bag and pulled out his pocket fisherman — a fishing rod and reel and hook, all in a nice little package. He pressed a button and then cast the line up the cliff face. The hook caught on the top of the cliff.

RJ pulled the line to make sure it would hold his weight. Then he hit another button, and the line retracted, pulling him right up the face of the cliff.

Five minutes later, he was inside Vincent's cave.

And inside the entrance, lit by moonlight, was a perfect bag of potato chips.

It was even bigger than the one in the vending machine.

RJ tiptoed in and picked up the bag. It rustled gently. He smiled at it. Then he looked up to see another bag of chips . . . and another!

He picked up the second bag, and then the third. He looked around to see if there was a fourth. And that's when he saw it.

Inside the cave was a mountain of junk food — a gigantic, glorious pile of edibles, sitting in and spilling out of a shiny red wagon.

RJ's eyes glittered. He moved towards the food, drooling slightly.

That's for me, he thought.

Suddenly, Vincent snorted. Then he reared up and shook his shaggy head.

RJ froze. It couldn't be time for Vincent to wake up . . . could it?

Vincent stretched. Then he flopped down on the floor of the cave again, right in front of RJ. He snored loudly.

RJ started to breathe again.

He stared over Vincent at the mound of food.

Just take what you need, he reminded himself. *Just take what you need . . . .*

It was good raccoon advice, passed along from his great-grandfather to his grandfather to his father. You were never supposed to take more than you needed. That way, nothing big and furry with lots of teeth would come chasing after you.

The problem was, RJ never listened to advice from anyone — especially his relatives.

A few minutes later, he stood back to admire his handiwork.

Every last bit of the food in the cave was neatly piled on the red wagon. Perched on top was a blue cooler.

Vincent snorted in his sleep, turned over, and flung a paw over his head.

RJ hit a switch. Under the red wagon, a giant airline raft inflated. The red wagon and all the food lifted off and gently floated over Vincent. It landed with a thud just inside the cave entrance.

Brilliant, RJ thought, *if I say so myself.*

Vincent snorted again. RJ held his breath.

Vincent hugged his paws to his furry chest and snored loudly.

RJ picked up a few boxes of cookies that had fallen off the wagon and tossed them onto the giant food pile. He turned. And that's when he saw it.

A cardboard can of potato chips, cuddled in Vincent's paws.

These were RJ's absolutely favorite potato chip . . . which meant they were his absolutely favorite food.

He stared at the can. He looked over at the

mountain of food on the red wagon. He looked back at the can again.

He couldn't resist.

He looked around the cave. In the corner, he saw an empty coffee cup.

He scurried over and picked it up. Then, very, very carefully, he moved over to Vincent.

Very, very carefully, he slid the cardboard can of chips out of Vincent's paws, replacing it with the coffee cup. The sleeping Vincent would never know the difference.

Vincent muttered something in his sleep and clutched at the coffee cup.

RJ smiled.

He backed away, looking down at the chips can. The picture of a stack of perfect potato chips made his mouth water.

Just one chip for the road, he thought . . .

Carefully, RJ lifted the pop-top on the can.

Pssssssssssh. A tiny wisp of air escaped from the can.

One of Vincent's yellow eyes popped open.

RJ gulped.

Vincent yawned, his teeth glinting in a strip of moonlight. He sat up and opened his other eye. He took in RJ and then the red wagon, piled high with goodies.

"RJ?" he growled.

"Uh . . . no?" RJ tried, starting to back up.

"The moon's not full. You woke me up a week early?"

Vincent stood up. He towered over the cowering raccoon.

"Oh, no," he said. "Don't tell me you're dumb enough to actually try and steal my stuff? RJ, I'm gonna have to kill you."

RJ backed up.

"Please," he stammered. "I'm just a desperate guy trying to feed his family."

Vincent snorted. "You don't have a family."

RJ swallowed. "I meant a family of one. Me."

Vincent took a giant step towards him.

RJ backed up some more. "Okay, wait, wait, wait! Look, it's still in your cave," he blabbered. "So technically, the stuff isn't stolen —"

Squeak.

RJ backed into the red wagon.

The wagon started to roll. It rolled out of the cave. Then it rolled to the edge of the cliff . . . and rolled right over.

Bang! Clunk! Crash!

"Ahhhhhh!" RJ gasped.

"Oh, no!" Vincent shrieked. "Noooo . . . slow down, slow down . . . stop!!!"

The wagon hit the ground at the base of the cliff and kept on rolling. It rolled across the highway and stopped just in front of the rest-stop.

The blue cooler on top wobbled a bit. But nothing happened. Every bit of food remained neatly stacked on the wagon.

Vincent breathed a sigh of relief.

"That was close —" he began.

A giant eighteen-wheeler zoomed down the highway and slammed into the little red wagon, scattering bits of metal and torn and broken packages of food everywhere.

Vincent's eyes turned an ugly shade of red.

He turned to RJ and roared.

RJ took off. Vincent chased him down the cliff face, screaming.

"You back-stabbing little bandit!"

Vincent caught up with RJ outside the rest stop. He picked the raccoon up in his giant paw, opened his mouth, and started to put RJ into it.

"Vincent, wait!" RJ yelled. "Please don't eat

me!" He could see his nose reflected in Vincent's molars. "I can get it all back!"

Vincent stopped.

"That's right!" RJ babbled. "If you eat me, *you'd* have to do it. But I can get it — all of it."

Vincent stared at RJ.

"My red wagon?" he asked, squeezing RJ.

"Redder!" RJ said. *"Owww!"*

"The blue cooler?" Vincent went on, squeezing a bit harder.

"Blue cooler, on my list," RJ gasped. "Gotta be blue?"

"Yes," Vincent said. "And I want my potato chips. I love those things . . . the way they fit so perfectly on your tongue."

"'Course you do, 'course you do," RJ jabbered. "And I'm gonna get you the giant picnic pack family-fun size."

Vincent's eyes gleamed. "They have that?"

"I'm pretty sure," RJ said.

Vincent nodded slowly and thought for a moment.

"Okay, RJ," he said finally. "Here's the deal. My hibernation ends when that moon is full." He gestured up towards the sky with a pawful of gleaming claws.

"So I'm going back to sleep. And when I wake up — ALL my stuff had better be right back where it was."

"In one week?" RJ gulped. "That's impossible for just one guy —"

Vincent squeezed even harder.

"A week's perfect," RJ said quickly. "I'll hire a temp. Maybe a few temps!"

"Full moon, all my stuff — and don't even think about running away. Because if you do, I'll hunt you down and kill you," Vincent said simply.

Vincent dropped RJ to the ground, turned around, and began padding back towards his cave.

RJ looked up at the sky. A sliver of moon grinned down at him.

"What are you laughing at?" he muttered.

Then he looked over at Vincent's broad, furry back.

"Okay, okay, buddy!" he called after Vincent. "You just rest easy, alright, 'cause I'm on it. Hey, in a week from now, we're gonna be laughing about this thing, huh? *Heh-heh . . . heh-heh! Boo-hoo-hoo!*"

RJ started to sob.

He turned and banged his head against the vending machine. The bag of potato chips that had been stuck in it plopped gently down into the opening.

RJ stared at the bag. Then he sighed, picked it up, and walked slowly away.

How was one little raccoon going to collect all that food and get it back to Vincent in just one week?

He was doomed.

TWO

RJ stood on the edge of the highway, staring at the remains of Vincent's food. A few tattered plastic wrappers drifted by.

Maybe there's something I can recover from this mess, he thought.

He scampered across the highway, looking for anything that looked edible. A smashed can of chips caught his eye. He picked it up and turned it upside down . . . but all that was left were crumbs.

On the other side of the highway was a Trendy's fast-food restaurant. A few food containers sat in front of the restaurant on a picnic bench. *Maybe there's food there!* RJ thought.

He raced over, dodging another eighteen-wheeler on the way, and looked inside the containers. But they were empty.

So was a nearby trash can.

RJ's shoulders slumped. *This is hopeless,* he thought. *I'm a dead raccoon.*

He started to walk along the highway, staring at his toes. *I wonder who'll come to my funeral. For that matter, I wonder if I'll have a funeral. I hardly know anybody around here.*

Maybe Vincent will organize a memorial service. After all, if he invites anybody, they'll have to come . . . or else.

A page of newsprint blew into RJ's face. He peeled it off and looked at it.

Two ads caught his eye — one for a red wagon and one for a blue cooler.

RJ frowned. Then he stared at the newspaper, thinking hard.

Something was brewing in his small but clever brain.

He looked around. A little ahead of him on the highway was a big green sign that said EL RANCHO CAMELOT ESTATES. On the sign was a picture of a man and a little girl, grilling some food behind a large suburban house.

Food, RJ thought. *Food and a red wagon and a blue cooler. I know who has that stuff.*

People have that stuff! And people live there . . . in that Rancho Camelot place!

A nearby fence caught his eye, and he trotted over to it. He peered through the slats.

Lights from a bunch of houses glittered back at him.

RJ slipped through the slats and headed for the lights.

Somewhere not too far away, snow was melting.

A drop of it hit the nose of Verne, a turtle who was hibernating peacefully inside a hollow log.

Verne woke up with a start.

"Oooh, boy. That's cold!" he said.

He crawled out of the log and looked around.

Winter was ending, and the world was a beautiful place. Bright blue crocuses popped up through melting snowbanks. Thawing mounds of snow hung off trees and bushes. Sunlight glinted on the remaining patches of white, making everything sparkle.

Verne turned back to the hollow log. Inside the log a group of animals were still sleeping. These were Verne's friends, but more than that they were his family. Sharing a cozy log all winter made a group close. "Hey, everyone!" he yelled. "Wake up! Hibernation's over!"

A pile of leaves inside the log exploded as Hammy, a squirrel, shot up from under it and darted towards Verne.

"Morning!" Hammy chirped.

"Morning, Hammy," Verne said.

"I gotta go wee-wee!" Hammy explained. He zipped away. Hammy had more energy than anyone else in the forest, even after he'd just awakened from three months of sound sleep.

"Do what you have to do," Verne called after him.

He turned back to the log. "Okay, anyone else? Let's go, alright, the rest of you. Come on, everybody, wake up. It's spring. And you know what that means — it means there are only 274 days left till winter. Come on. We've got to get going."

Ziiiip! Hammy appeared again.

"Finished!" he said cheerily. "Oooh, no . . . wait."

He disappeared again. He was back a second later.

"Now I'm done!"

Verne sighed and turned back to the log. "Let's go," he called. "Come on, everybody. Wake up. Don't make me come in there."

A black tail with a white stripe down the middle appeared from under the leaf pile.

"Y'all better listen," said a muffled voice. "I've been holding something in all winter, and I'm about to let it out."

A second later, five porcupines and two possums exploded from out of the pile, leaving the owner of the tail — a skunk named Stella — curled up in the leaves. She smiled up at Verne and winked.

"Thank you, Stella," Verne said.

Stella shrugged. "Oh, I can clear a room, Verne — *that* much I can do."

She picked herself up, brushed a few dead leaves out of her fur, and stepped out of the log as Verne trotted back in. He headed for the very back.

Outside, the porcupine kids — Quillo, Bucky, and Spike — ran under and around the feet of their mother, Penny. The two possums — Ozzie and his daughter, Heather — stretched and yawned.

Lou, the porcupine kids' dad, sniffed the crisp, fresh air.

"Goood morning, everyone!" he said. "Just a super-duper morning, eh?"

Penny rubbed her nose. "Aw, jeepers," she muttered.

Lou stared at her. "Whoa," he said. "Not lookin' so good around the eyes there, hon."

Penny glared back at him. "Oh, the kids just woke me up every two or three weeks is all. Of course, you were sleeping like a log in the log there . . . ."

Lou gave her a quick hug. "You know what? How 'bout I take the day shift?" he suggested.

Penny smiled. "Oh, Lou, that'd be just super!"

Lou turned to the kids. "Alright," he said. "You heard your mother, and now you listen to me. Shape up there!"

"Whoo-hooo!" the kids yelled. Quillo took a flying leap and slammed into Lou, knocking him onto the ground.

Hammy zipped up to Stella.

"Where's the food?" he jabbered. "Is there any food left I'm really hungry so is there any food left in there, huh?"

Heather wandered over. "We ate all the food,

Hammy. During the winter? So we've gotta go get some more now."

Hammy nodded. "Oh, rrrrrrright! I buried some nuts in the woods and I know where they are and I'll be right back byeeeeee!"

Ziiiiip! He zipped away again, shaking loose a small clump of icy snow from a branch overhead. The snow fell on Ozzie.

"*Waaaa!*" shrieked the surprised possum. He clutched his chest and dropped down dead.

All the other animals stared at him. Lou rolled his eyes. Quillo giggled.

Heather smiled apologetically and moved towards him.

"Dad," she whispered urgently. "It was just snow."

Ozzie's eyes popped open.

"But it could have been a predator," he whispered.

Heather heaved a sigh and reached down, pulling Ozzie to his feet.

"Dad. Isn't playing dead a little . . . weak?" she said.

Ozzie shook his head. "Heather, how many times

must I say it — playing possum is what we *do*. We die so that we can live! You die today, so —"

Verne stepped out of the log. Behind his back, he held a branch with a clump of berries on it.

"Uh, excuse me, everybody —" he began.

He was interrupted by a giant, spiky ball of porcupine. It was Lou, rolling down the snowy slope, covered in his three screaming kids.

"I'm the boss of you, okay, so just calm down!" Lou hollered.

"Daddy!" yelled Bucky.

"Get offa me!" shouted Spike.

"Wheee!" giggled Quillo.

"I don't wanna hear anymore —" Lou bellowed.

Penny smiled at her husband as he rolled by with the kids. She turned to Stella.

"That's what we need to find you this year, don'tcha know," she said. "A good fella."

"A good fella?" Stella said quietly.

"Uh-oh." Penny backed up a step.

"A good *fella*!?" Stella repeated, louder this time.

Penny shook her head. "Aw, jeepers, here we go. . . ."

"Why," said Stella loudly, planting her paws on

her hips, "does everyone think I need a man? When you look like a nest and smell like last year's eggs, you learn to get by without! So when you find a fella who's decent, good with kids, and has no sense of smell . . . call me."

Verne was still trying to get everyone's attention. "Um, hello. . . . Penny . . . please, Lou . . ."

The porcupine ball rolled back the other way.

"Mom!" Bucky whined. "Quillo started it!"

"I don't care who started it," Lou grumbled.

Verne held the berry branch over his head.

"Ahem." He cleared his throat.

Everyone looked over at him, then up at the berries.

"Oh, look!" Penny said excitedly. "Food!"

Verne shook his head. "Well," he began, "I think you know, uh, what this means —"

Just then, Hammy popped up in front of Verne. He looked terrified.

"Verne," he gasped.

"Just a minute, Hammy," Verne said. He turned back to the others. "This means," he went on, gesturing to the berries, "that we made it . . . with leftovers."

He handed a berry to Heather.

"Thanks," Heather said, munching.

"Verne!" Hammy shook Verne's shell.

"Not finished yet, Hammy," Verne said kindly. He turned and handed a berry each to Penny and Lou.

"Morning, Lou. Penny," he said.

"Thanks," said Penny, popping the berry into her mouth.

Verne turned to the porcupine kids, giving Quillo, Bucky, and Spike each a berry. "So what I want to tell you all," he went on, "is another successful hibernation —"

"VERNE!" Hammy shrieked.

Verne handed Hammy a berry.

"I'm not done yet, Hammy," he said sternly. "If you have to go again, just go." He turned back to the other animals. "So as I was saying, a successful hibernation thanks to all of our hard work last fall. *But* . . . we cut it a little close, so this year we need to make sure that we fill the log —"

"All the way to the top," Ozzie finished.

Verne nodded approvingly. "Exactly. All the way to the top. So when we go out to forage, I'd like you to remember . . ."

"I love this part," Lou murmured.

"Eat one . . ." Verne began.

"Save two!" the other animals chorused.

"Right," Verne said seriously.

"Never changes," Lou said approvingly. "Super, Verne. Really super."

Verne smiled. Then, finally, he turned to Hammy.

"Okay, Hammy," he said.

By this point, Hammy was sucking a bit of berry from between his teeth. Food always made him feel so much better.

"Hammy?"

"Huh?" Hammy said.

"What is it?"

"What is what?" Hammy looked confused.

"What is it you want to tell me?" Verne said patiently.

"Hmm? Oh! Oh! Oh! What was it, what was it, what was it, wait, right on the tip of my tongue . . . oh yeah! There's a weird thing over there I've never seen before. It's really scary. Follow me."

Hammy zipped off. Verne and the other animals stared at him for a second. Then they followed.

Behind them, RJ popped out from behind a bush. He blinked. *Hmmm. Animals,* he thought. *I wonder if any of them want a temp job. . . .*

Verne and the others caught up with Hammy at the edge of the woods. RJ was right behind them, keeping out of sight.

"So, Hammy. What weird thing?" Verne asked.

Hammy pointed up.

Verne and the others looked in the direction he was pointing.

Verne's mouth dropped open.

"Oh," he said quietly. "*That* weird thing."

The other animals stared in horror.

There in front of them was a giant hedge. A hedge that hadn't been there when they'd gone to sleep the autumn before.

Penny pulled her kids to her. Lou gulped. Ozzie started to collapse, but Heather pinched him.

The hedge was big, bright green, and neatly trimmed.

Verne looked left and then right. The hedge stretched out in both directions as far as he could see.

Hammy darted down its length for a while. He passed RJ in a flurry of leaves and dirt. RJ, startled, scampered behind a nearby tree. He hid there as Hammy zipped back and stood in front of Verne.

"It never ends," Hammy said solemnly.

He raced along it in the other direction, th raced back again.

"It never ends that way, too," he added.

Verne stepped closer to the hedge. The other animals moved with him.

They stared up at it.

"Whoa," said Heather.

"Jeepers, Lou," Penny muttered.

"Yeah, jeepers is the word there, hon." Lou nodded.

Stella stared. "Man, that's big."

"What is this thing?" Heather asked.

She reached out to touch it.

"Heather, no!" Ozzie grabbed her paw.

"I'm scared," Spike said in a little voice.

"Me, too, Mama!" Quillo sniffed.

Penny clutched her children to her. "Shh, shh . . . it's okay. It's just a . . ." She turned to her husband. "What *is* this thing, Lou?"

"I, well . . . it's a . . . it's a . . . it's . . . Verne?" Lou turned to the turtle.

So did all the other animals.

Verne stroked his chin. "Well," he began, "it's obviously some kind of . . . bush?"

Penny shook her head. "I would be a lot less afraid of it if I just knew what it was called."

"Let's call it Steve!" Hammy said brightly.

"Steve?" Verne stared at the squirrel.

"It's a pretty name," Hammy said defensively.

"Steve sounds nice," admitted Heather.

"Yeah." Penny agreed. "I'm a lot less scared of Steve."

Ozzie bowed down to the hedge. "Oh, great and powerful Steve — what do you want?"

Steve was silent.

"I don't think it can speak," Verne said.

"*I heard that, young man!*" came a voice from behind the hedge.

"*Ahhhhh!*" The animals gasped and huddled together. Ozzie fell flat on his back and played dead. He motioned for Heather to do the same. She rolled her eyes and nudged him gently with her rear paw.

"*You get over here right now!*" the voice went on.

"Okay," Hammy said obediently. He moved towards the hedge.

"Hammy!" Verne whispered frantically. "Get back here!"

Hammy turned. "But Steve is angry!"

Verne shook his head. "I think the voice came

from the other side of Steve — I mean the bush — I mean, gee — Look, there's only one way we're gonna find out what this thing is and what this is all about. I'm gonna go check it out."

Verne stepped bravely forward. Penny reached out to stop him. The others held their breath. Then Verne tripped over a loose branch and fell . . . right into the hedge!

"*Ahhhhhh!!!*" the animals screamed.

"STEVE — ATE — VERNE!" Ozzie fainted dead away.

Stella stomped over to the hedge, furious.

"All right, Steve," she said. "You brought this on yourself!"

She turned her rear end towards the hedge and lifted her tail.

"Stella, don't!" Verne hissed, poking his head out of the hedge. "I'm not eaten. I just tripped. I'm gonna go over there. Just don't anybody move!"

Stella dropped her tail. The others stared.

Verne disappeared back into the hedge again.

RJ scampered up the tree he'd been hiding behind. He peered over the hedge, waiting to see what would happen next.

This is going to be interesting, he thought.

THREE

Verne nervously stepped through the hedge and into a backyard.

He was standing in Rancho Camelot Estates — a new suburban housing development that had been built while he and the other animals were asleep.

Of course, he didn't know that's what it was. To him, it was as if he had stepped onto the moon.

Rancho Camelot Estates consisted of about a hundred brand-new human homes, all with nice new patios and green backyards.

Verne was standing in one of the backyards, which happened to belong to Gladys Sharp, president of the Rancho Camelot Estates Homeowners' Association.

Verne studied the carefully trimmed green lawn.

Every blade of grass was exactly two inches tall. It looked strange and unnatural.

A dragonfly fluttered towards him.

"Oh!" Verne said, relieved. At least this was something he recognized. "Hey there, little —"

The dragonfly flew into a bug zapper. It was instantly fried.

"Fella," Verne finished lamely as the smoking dragonfly dropped at his feet.

As Verne backed away, he tripped over a flattened turtle-shaped stepping-stone.

"*Ahhh!*" he squealed, bumping into what appeared to be the back half of a dog digging in the yard. Verne backed away from it and stumbled into a big green plastic toad.

"Hi," Verne said tentatively to the toad.

The toad opened its mouth as if to answer. But instead, it sprayed a powerful jet of water smack into Verne, slamming him back into a stone column.

A shiny reflector ball that was on top of the column teetered back and forth, then rolled off and slammed into the ground. It started rolling towards him.

Verne glanced over his shoulder at the ball. A

hundred shiny reflections of him stared back. Terrified, he yanked his head, arms, legs and tail into his shell just as the ball rolled right over him, flipping him into the air.

Unfortunately, he landed on the ball. He rolled along on top of it.

"*Whoa, whoa, whoa, whoa, whoa, whoa* —" he yelled.

SMACK!

He and the ball hit the leg of a barbecue grill that was sitting on the patio. A big shiny spatula whacked into his shell, sending him spinning off the ball.

He grabbed for the spatula and hung on, but it pulled free of the grill, and he crashed to the ground. He started to crawl away, stepping over a garden hose.

As he did, he heard a sound. He looked up, and his eyes widened. Above him, a gleaming assortment of sharp-looking grilling tools were falling from the grill — and coming straight towards him!

"*Ahhhhhh!*" he shrieked, sucking his head and limbs into his shell again — and just in time. The knives and tongs rained down, narrowly missing him.

One of the knives landed on the hose, slicing it in half.

A spray of water burst out of the hose, sending it snaking into the air — with Verne holding on for dear life. The hose whipped back and forth, almost shaking the poor turtle out of his shell.

Verne struggled to hold on, but it was no use. Before he knew it, he was flying over the garden fence.

He landed on a plastic SUV pedal toy, sending a mini coffee cup and a toy cell phone flying up into the air. The SUV rolled off, with Verne inside. The sippy cup and cell phone landed in his front hands.

Looking just like a small turtle commuter, Verne rolled onto the street in his mini SUV, clutching the cell phone and sippy cup.

Unfortunately, a human-size SUV, driven by Gladys Sharp, was approaching in the same lane.

Verne sucked himself up into his shell in a panic as Gladys drove towards him.

"I can talk," she was yelling into her own, human-size cell phone. "I'm driving."

"*Ahhhhhh!*" Verne shrieked, shutting his eyes tight as the shadow of the huge SUV engulfed him.

The SUV zoomed down the street, leaving Verne still sliding across the road. He slammed into a mailbox post just as two BMX bikes zoomed up. As he careened into the street again, the bikes rolled right over him, flipping him into the middle of the road and spinning him in circles.

When he finally came to a stop, he opened his eyes and peered out of his shell.

A hockey puck slid up right next to him.

Verne frowned. What was *that*?

But there was no time to figure it out. Three roller-hockey players skated over and, mistaking Verne for their puck, slap-shot him over a fence, through the hedge, and —

"Verne!" Lou yelled.

Verne hit the ground with a thud on the other side of the hedge and skidded to a stop.

His friends rushed over to him.

"Jeepers!" Penny said.

"Are you okay?" Heather asked.

"What was over there?" Ozzie wanted to know.

Verne gasped, out of breath. "I think . . . it was . . . humans," he finally said.

The animals all looked at one another in dismay. "Humans."

Verne nodded. "They must have come while we were hibernating," he said. "And they — it was awful — they had wheels on their feet and they had these sticks and they were whacking me with these sticks like it was some sort of sick game!"

"You should have died," Ozzie said firmly. "You should have laid down and died!"

Heather frowned. "Dad . . ."

In the tree above them, RJ shook his head and went back to writing up his list — the list of goodies he needed to pay back Vincent and save his life.

Nuts, he thought.

Down below, Verne was talking again.

"That's not the worst part. Half the forest is gone. The oak trees and the berry bushes, they're just . . . they're just . . . *gone.*"

The animals stood there, stunned.

"Jeepers," Penny said again.

She pulled the kids close as Lou put his arm around her shoulder.

"What'll we do for food?" Stella wanted to know.

Verne blinked. "I don't know. But here's what I do know. We will be fine as long as no one goes over Steve" — he pointed back at the hedge — "*ever* again."

There was a noise from up in the tree. The animals raised their heads.

"It's called a hedge, and it is not to be feared, my amphibious friend," said a voice above them. "It is the gateway to the good life."

Verne squinted as he stared up through the leaves. "Uh, I'm a reptile, actually," he explained. "But you know, it's a common mistake. And you are . . . ?"

RJ slid down a branch and onto the ground.

"Oh," he said, bowing elegantly. "Where are my manners? I'm RJ. Now, please don't think I'm prying, but I think I can shed a little light on what this whole hedge situation is about."

The animals looked at one another.

"You see," RJ went on smoothly, pulling out a map, "what was once mere wilderness is now fifty-four acres of man-made, manicured, air-conditioned paradise. Except for *that* little-bitty speck."

He pointed at a tiny point of green on the map. The animals crowded around to look.

"You are here," RJ said.

"Huh? What?" The animals stared in disbelief.

"No, no, that's a good thing," RJ said, jabbing his finger at the map. "Because if you're hurtin' for food, here is where you wanna be. You're hibernators, right? You gather up a bunch of food, store it away for the winter?"

Hammy nodded vigorously. "Uh-huh. We fill the log."

RJ turned to stare at the log. "You fill this log? Really, this one right here?"

"All the way to the top," Ozzie said proudly.

"Ozzie," Verne began.

RJ took a tape measure out of his bag and quickly measured the log.

"Let me ask you," he said, turning and flipping the tape measure back into its little case. "How long does it take . . . you know . . . to fill the log?"

"Two hundred seventy-four days," Heather said.

"Whoa!" RJ stared at her. "Ever done it in a week?"

"Heh-heh. A week?" Verne said. "That's impossible."

"For one guy, yeah." RJ smiled. "For you guys, maybe. But for all of us, working together . . . oh, man, we could get all the food we want . . . right over that hedge."

Verne's eyes widened. "What? Over there?"

RJ nodded. "Yeah. Because where there's a hedge, there's a suburb, and where there's a suburb, there are people. And where there are people, there is *food*."

"How much food?" Heather wanted to know.

"Loads of food. *Heaps* of food. Food out the wazoo!" RJ opened his arms wide.

Verne stepped in front of RJ. "Well," he said, "whatever kind of food comes out of a wazoo, I really don't think we're interested in eating —"

Lou interrupted him. "I don't know. The guy's making a lot of sense to me. I think we should listen."

Penny took her husband's arm. "Yeah," she added. "I'm okay with wazoo food there."

Verne shot her a look. "No, you're not. The tail is tingling. . . ."

The other animals stared at him.

"Oh. The tail."

"There you go, then."

"Why didn't you say so?"

RJ scratched his head. "Hold on, hold on. The what is what?"

Verne turned to RJ. "Every time I feel like something's wrong, my tail tingles."

RJ looked serious. "I'm sure that's a very

sophisticated warning system you've got there, but believe me — you're Verne, right?"

Verne nodded.

"Well, Verne," RJ went on. "This isn't something you need to be afraid of."

Verne turned his back to RJ and the others. There were tire tracks all over his shell.

The animals gasped.

"Well, I *am* afraid," he said stiffly. "And with good reason. These are not birthmarks."

"Ah," RJ said as he pulled an electric toothbrush out of his golf bag and began cleaning Verne's shell. "That's because you went over there without a guide, Verne. See, I know the ins and outs, and the best time to go over there is between the hours of seven and ten P.M. . . . that's prime time. When humans are sitting there bloated in front of the TV, like pythons that just ate a goat."

Verne rolled his eyes. "You know, thanks, JR —"

"RJ," RJ corrected him.

"Whatever," Verne went on. "Thanks for stopping by — but we're not interested."

"Not interested in the most delicious food you've ever tasted? Come on —"

"*No!*" Verne interrupted him. "Not interested!"

RJ shrugged. "Okay . . . I understand. This is something that you're just not open to."

RJ pulled a bag of chips out of his golf bag. He pointed it at the other animals and then . . . *poof!!* . . . opened it.

A delicious smell wafted towards them, as it got closer it seemed to get stronger until it enveloped them all. The porcupine kids were knocked off their feet while the rest of the animals felt their fur ruffle as cheesy goodness enveloped them. Noses twitched. Mouths watered.

"Whoa!"

"Jeepers!"

"Wow!"

"What . . . is . . . *that*?"

RJ began passing out chips. "That, my friend, is a magical combination of corn flour, dehydrated cheese solids, BHA, BHT, and good old MSG — aka, the chip. Nacho cheese flavor."

Sounds of chewing filled the forest. The animals licked their lips.

"Can I have some more, RJ?"

"Over here, RJ!"

"Please, RJ!"

"Yeah. Those were good!"

RJ grinned. "It's *all* good. And we're going over there, tonight!"

All of the animals — all except Verne — nodded enthusiastically.

"Count me in!"

"Me too!"

"Me three!"

Verne stared at RJ. His tail was tingling like crazy.

This wasn't good. It wasn't good at all.

FOUR

"Welcome . . . to suburbia."

RJ ushered his little tour group into Gladys Sharp's backyard. Right on cue, the sprinklers spurted to life.

The animals gasped.

RJ swished his tail across a motion sensor and lights twinkled on, bathing everything in a golden glow.

It was amazing.

Every blade of grass really was exactly the same height. Each droplet of water from the sprinklers glistened like a tiny, perfect diamond.

The animals stood and stared at the green, manicured perfection of it all.

"Whoa."

"This is nice."

RJ waved his hand expansively. "Go ahead," he told them. "Check it out."

Quillo, Bucky, and Spike noticed the shiny reflecting ball that had rolled after Verne. They raced over and stared into it, making funny faces.

"Hey, Mom!" they called to Penny. "Look at us, look at us!"

"Jeepers," Penny said, staring in astonishment at a potted cactus. She poked at it gently with a paw.

Verne walked over to RJ and watched as the animals explored the backyard.

"How's that tail, Verne?" RJ asked jovially.

"Listen," Verne replied in a tight voice. "If anybody in this family gets hurt, I'm holding you personally responsible."

RJ put his arm around Verne's shell. "Hey . . . they're having a good time. I'll take responsibility for *that*."

Verne shook his head and pulled it into his shell as the lawn sprinklers shot streams of water into the sky like an elaborate fountain.

"Whoa, look at that," Ozzie murmured.

"This is neat!" said Heather.

Lou stepped up to Verne.

"Verno?" he said.

Verne's head popped out of his shell.

"I took a few clippings to do a little comparison," Lou said, showing Verne some blades of grass. "And look at this. This grass seems to be greener over here than it is back where we live —"

Ozzie frowned. "Verne, are you certain you came to the same place?"

"Yeah," Stella added. "'Cause, you know, the raccoon said —"

Verne interrupted. "Okay, enough about him. I get it. So he can do a couple of tricks — I mean, it's not like he can walk on water!"

"Hey, everybody!" RJ yelled. "This way to the food!"

RJ hopped to the edge of the pool and across a couple of pool rafts. It looked like he was walking on the water. Sort of.

The animals stared. Then they scampered after him.

Verne shook his head and sighed.

RJ led them up to the driveway. A large, shadowy vehicle was standing there.

"What is *that*?" Hammy whispered.

"That is an SUV," RJ explained. "Humans ride

around in it because they are slowly losing their ability to walk."

Penny stared up at the looming shape.

"Jeepers," she said. "It's so big!"

Lou scratched his head. "How many humans fit in there?"

RJ blinked. "Usually? One."

At that moment, a human female opened the kitchen door and headed for the SUV.

"Hi," she was saying into a cordless phone. "This is Gladys Sharp? Your president? Of the Homeowner's Association? Right."

The animals all froze.

"Jeepers," Penny whispered. "What is that?"

"Easy, easy," said RJ reassuringly. "Don't worry. That's just a human being. And they are just as scared of us as we are of them. Now, if a human does happen to see you, just lie down, roll over, and give yourself a good licking. They love it."

The animals shuddered.

When Gladys got to the SUV, she opened the door, reached in and grabbed a bag of groceries.

". . . the most important thing I'm ever gonna say to you," she said into the phone. "See, according to the charter, the grass is supposed to be two inches, and yours is more like two point four."

Gladys slammed the SUV's door shut and headed back into her house.

"Could we just get the food and go?" Verne muttered. "Really, do they have it or not?"

RJ chuckled. "Didn't you see it?" he asked. "It was in the bag! They've always got food with them. We eat to live . . . these guys live to eat. Let me show you what I'm talking about."

RJ zipped out of Gladys's backyard and headed for the house just next door. The other animals followed.

RJ stopped in front of a big picture window. He and the animals stared inside at a large TV set.

On the TV, a human was shoving a burger into his mouth.

"The human mouth," RJ began, "is called a 'pie hole.'"

He turned and clambered up a tree. The others climbed up after him, looking around at the scores of gleaming new houses.

In a living room window across the road, a human male entered and sat down in a recliner.

"The human being," RJ went on, gesturing to the seated man, "is also called a 'couch potato.'"

Next to the living room, the animals could see into a kitchen. A woman hung up a telephone.

"That is a device to summon food," RJ explained.

Almost immediately, a pizza delivery man arrived at the front door of the house. He rang the doorbell.

The animals jumped at the sound.

"That is one of the many voices of food," RJ told them.

Footsteps could be heard inside the house. In a minute, the woman opened the door, and the pizza man handed her the pizza.

"That," RJ said, pointing to the front door, "is the portal for the passing of the food."

The pizza man hopped back on his motorbike, which was piled high with more pizzas.

"That," RJ went on, "is one of the many food transportation vehicles."

A pizza truck passed the motorbike, going in the opposite direction. Then a hamburger truck drove by.

"Humans bring the food, take the food, ship the food," RJ explained.

A large truck shaped like a taco drove past. Two people dressed as ice-cream cones walked by, followed by an ice-cream truck.

"They drive the food, they wear the food."

In a backyard nearby, a man was grilling hot dogs.

"That gets the food hot," RJ said, pointing to the grill.

Nearby, a cooler was filled with drinks.

"That keeps the food cold," RJ said.

In another backyard, a young boy broke a piñata, and candy came showering down.

"Ahhh," Verne murmured.

"Hey. What do you know?" RJ grinned. *"Food!"*

A family across the way sat around their table and started to say grace. RJ waved his paw at them.

"That is the altar where they worship food."

A man popped a tablet into a glass and drank it down, making a face.

"That's what they eat when they've eaten too much food," RJ said.

A man took a bite out of an ear of corn. Another man popped a steak onto his black eye. A woman relaxed in her tub, cucumber slices over her eyes. A couple of construction workers opened some soda cans and sprayed soda at one another, laughing.

"Food. Food. Food. FOOD!" RJ sang out.

"So, you think they have enough food?" RJ proclaimed. "Well, they don't. They have TOO MUCH!!!"

46

And what do they do with the stuff they don't eat? They put it in gleaming silver cans — just for us."

RJ scampered over to a group of trash cans that were standing behind Gladys Sharp's home. The others followed.

RJ kicked one over.

Food spilled out — more and more and more food.

The animals stared, mesmerized.

"Sweet jeepers!" Penny breathed.

"Dig in!" RJ said happily.

The animals dove into the piles and piles of food.

"Mmmm . . . good, isn't it?" RJ said, coming up for air, a pizza crust stuck to his nose.

Bits of food flew everywhere as the animals gorged.

"Wow!"

"Share there, everyone, share."

"Oh, my!"

Verne picked something up carefully and stared at it.

"Uh, that's a diaper, Verne," RJ told him. "I'd advise against it. That stuff *does* come out of a wazoo."

Verne made a face and dropped the diaper.

Hammy put his mouth over the opening of a can of cheese and squirted. The gooey orange stuff shot into his mouth and out of his nose.

"So, what do you think?" RJ said. "Was I right or was I right? And these things are just the scraps! Wait till you see what comes in the boxes and the packages and the cans! I'm telling you, folks, you stick with me and in one week, we will gather enough food to . . . to . . . to . . . feed a bear!"

BEEP!

A fat Persian cat stepped through an automatic pet door into the backyard.

"Halt!" the cat screeched. "Intruders! Intruders! Get out, all of you!"

The animals stepped back.

"MEEEOOOOOOW!"

The back door flew open. There, silhouetted in the light, stood the towering figure of . . . Gladys Sharp.

"What is it, baby?" she said to the cat.

Then she noticed the animals near her garbage cans.

"AAAAAAAAAAAAHHHHGH!" she shrieked.

The animals all dropped onto their backs and started licking themselves.

IT'S...WELL, OBVIOUSLY IT'S SOME KIND OF BUSH.

I'D BE A LOT LESS AFRAID OF IT IF I KNEW WHAT IT WAS CALLED.

LET'S CALL IT STEVE!

STEVE SOUNDS NICE.

I'M A LOT LESS AFRAID OF STEVE.

IT'S A PRETTY NAME.

Porcupine Family

Ozzie & Heather

RJ

Hammy

Verne

"What . . . are . . . you . . . doing?" RJ yelled.

Lou looked up. "Well, you said we should lick our —"

"No!! Nix that. *RUUUUUUUNNNNN!*"

Gladys grabbed a broom that was near the door and started to swipe it at them.

"Run!!! Run!" the animals shouted to one another.

"Get outta here! Shoo!" cried Gladys, swinging the broom at Hammy, who was running around in circles with a mayonnaise jar on his head.

"To the hedge!" RJ yelled.

The animals scrambled for the hedge, with Gladys right behind them.

"Out of my yard! Disgusting vermin!" she screeched.

Two minutes later, the animals were on the other side of the hedge, breathless and panting.

"Verne was right," Penny gasped. "That was horrible. Stay close to me, kids."

"You guys okay?" Lou patted his offspring to make sure they hadn't broken anything. "You alright there, hon?"

"We'll find other food, right?" Heather babbled.

"See what I mean?" Verne's eyes glittered. "That's what I was talking about! Those humans don't want us around!"

RJ sniffed. "So we scared her and she overreacted," he said. "No biggie."

Verne stared at RJ. "No biggie? Oh, that is what *we* call a biggie."

RJ blinked. "Come on," he said. "Think about the food. It was worth it for that food, huh? That stuff is to die for!"

The other animals gasped. Ozzie fell down and played dead.

"Let me rephrase that . . ." RJ began.

"No," Verne snapped. "To die for. You nailed that part. Look, maybe our little forest life looks primitive to a guy with a bag . . ."

"Huh?" RJ said.

"But gee," Verne went on. "I think I speak for the whole family when I say — we want *nothing* to do with *anything* that's over that hedge."

Verne stared at RJ for a moment. Then he turned and walked away.

One by one, the other animals followed.

"Aw, c'mon," RJ pleaded.

"I'm done," Stella said over her shoulder.

Lou nodded. "Sure the food was good there, but is it worth it?"

RJ scampered after them. "You haven't even tried donuts yet! You wanna store fat? *That* is the way to store some fat. You'll be *sweatin'* through the winter!!"

"Hold my hand, Spike," Lou said, looking down at his son.

"Let's eat the bark, like Verne said," Heather said.

RJ shrugged. "Okay, alright, you, you guys sleep on it! Good idea. I'm gonna check back with you."

He turned away. "*Shoot,*" he muttered to himself.

He had to figure out a way to change their minds . . . or he was in big trouble. He needed their help to collect all of the food he owed Vincent.

Because if he couldn't feed the bear . . . then Vincent would have *him* for lunch.

FIVE

That night, up in a big oak tree, RJ pulled a piece of newspaper out of his golf bag to use as a blanket. He plumped up the golf bag to make a pillow.

It wasn't the most comfortable way to sleep . . . but he was used to it.

Down below, the animal family was saying good night.

"Good night, Heather."

"Good night, Verne."

"Good night, Ozzie."

"Good night, Verne."

"Good night, Lou."

"Good night, Penny."

"Good night, Bucky."

"Good night, Uncle Verne."

RJ sneezed, and his newspaper blew away.

Oh, shoot, he thought.

"Good night, Spike. Good night, Quillo."

"Good night, Uncle Verne."

RJ turned over, shivering. Suddenly he felt very alone.

He closed his eyes.

The sun rose. RJ's eyes began to open.

"Potato chips . . . cooler . . . wagon . . . redder," he muttered.

A giant bear paw grabbed him by the head and yanked him out of the tree.

It was Vincent!

"Time's up, RJ," Vincent said cheerfully.

"But . . . but I have six more days!" RJ gasped.

Vincent opened his gigantic mouth. Light gleamed on his sharp yellow teeth.

"NOOOOOOOO! AAAHHHHHHHH!" RJ screamed. Vincent's mouth got closer . . . and closer!!! His breath was terrible —

RJ's eyes snapped open. He sat bolt upright.

It was a beautiful day, and Vincent was nowhere to be seen.

"Whaa???" RJ moaned, patting himself. "Four paws . . . fur . . . still alive, still alive . . ."

He breathed a sigh of relief. It had been a dream.

But, he reminded himself, if he couldn't figure out a way to get Vincent's food back to him, it was a dream that would come true.

Squeak! Squeak! Squeak!

RJ stretched stiffly and looked out of the tree, over to where the noise was coming from.

He blinked and rubbed his eyes.

On the other side of the hedge was a red wagon, being pulled down the sidewalk by two girls in uniforms. The wagon was filled with colorful boxes of cookies.

Squeak! Squeak! Squeak!

The girls were talking, and RJ strained to hear them.

"So, what are you saying? You want *me* to take them to his house?

"No."

"Then what are you saying?"

"Jimmy was totally pushing me on the bus yesterday."

"He likes you."

"No way. He's a creep."

"Next time he shoves you, beat him up."

"Yes!"

"I'll just tell Bobby . . ."

The girls moved away. RJ scratched his head. He had no idea what they were talking about. But that food . . . oh, if only he could get his paws on it! And the red wagon . . . it was perfect!

Down below, the other animals were busy gathering food. But it didn't look very appetizing.

Stella was listlessly picking up sticks.

Hammy was trying to carve out a nacho chip–shaped piece of bark from a tree with his teeth. He grabbed a passing bumblebee and shook some yellow pollen onto the triangular piece of bark. It still didn't look very much like a nacho chip.

"Awww," he groaned. The bee flew away, grumbling.

Lou peeled off a piece of bark from another tree with his quills. He held it out to the kids.

"Okay, dive in," he said cheerfully. "Here it is!"

Spike looked at the bark and turned up his nose. "Yuck!" he said.

"I want a donut," Bucky whined.

"I want a pizza!" Quillo added.

"No you don't," said Penny.

Nearby, Verne was carrying an armload of grass

and bark over to the hollow log. He carefully placed them inside. Then he took a piece of bark and took a bite. He chewed hard.

The other animals stared at him.

"Okay," he said. "Granted it takes some time to chew. But that . . ." He swallowed. "That was very satisfying. And by the way, lots of fiber in there, too. Mmmm." He crunched some more. "Lots."

"I gotta admit . . . that does look tasty."

The animals turned. RJ smiled and nodded at them. While nobody was looking, Verne spit out the rest of the piece of bark.

"What are *you* doing here?" he asked RJ.

"I'm here to help you with your . . . foraging . . . thing," RJ replied. "Look, Verne, you said a word yesterday about your little gang here, starts with an 'f.' Do you remember what it was?"

"Family?" Verne said.

"Right, right, that," RJ answered, nodding vigorously. "You know, that got me right here." He pointed to his heart. "You see, Verne, I was never lucky enough to have a family of my own. At least, not since . . . the weed whacker incident."

All the animals blinked.

Hammy raced over to RJ.

"Oh, come here, you poor thing," he said, full of compassion. He put his arms around RJ and gave him a big hug. "That feels good, doesn't it?"

A tear dropped from RJ's eye. Just one . . . he didn't want to overdo it. He looked down at the ground.

Verne rolled his eyes. "Oh, brother," he muttered.

"Jeepers, Verne," Penny said gently. "Have a heart."

"We could always use the extra hand here, you know," Lou added.

"The weed wacker, Verne. The weed wacker," Hammy said, his little voice breaking. "Give the guy a chance."

Verne shook his head.

RJ looked up. "Okay," he said dramatically. "Not your problem. I'll . . . just go. This is me . . . going. Been nice, really nice getting to know you all. Hey, I'm sure I'll see you around the forest."

Hammy started to sniffle.

RJ smiled bravely. "Take care," he said.

He turned, his shoulders slumping. *If this doesn't get them, nothing will,* he thought. Then he started to stumble away.

All the other animals turned to Verne with pleading eyes.

"Alright, alright," Verne said finally, giving in. "Hey, RJ? You can stay."

RJ turned around and pumped his fist.

"Whoo-hoo!" he yelled. "C'mere, you big lug!"

He raced over to Verne and put his arms around the turtle, lifting him up in the air.

"No!" Verne started to say. But RJ interrupted him.

"I knew beneath this hard crispy outside, there was a soft center in there. Do you mind if I call you Uncle Verne?"

"With every bone in my body," Verne said stiffly.

RJ put him down. "Great!" he said. "Hey, can I work with Hammy?"

Without waiting for an answer, RJ walked over and put his arm around the little squirrel. And before Verne could say anything, RJ drew Hammy away from the others.

Hammy, flattered, puffed out his chest happily.

Verne stared after them, worried. Whatever RJ had to say, Hammy was sure to listen. And whatever RJ had to say, Verne was sure he was up to no good.

Hammy, however, had no such thoughts.

"Want me to show you what I do with my nuts?" he asked RJ eagerly.

"Very tempting, Hammy, very tempting," RJ said smoothly. "But first, I want to show you this."

He held out a cookie. Hammy sniffed. His eyes widened.

"You like this cookie?" RJ said.

"Oh, ho-ho-ho!" Hammy said. He reached for the cookie.

But before he could take it, RJ tossed it away.

"Well, this cookie's *junk*!" RJ said.

"I like a cookie!" Hammy whined.

RJ smiled. "Well, I know where we can get some cookies so valuable that they are hand-delivered by uniformed officers."

Hammy gasped.

"Come right this way," RJ said, pointing to a tree.

RJ and Hammy sat at the top of the tree, looking down over the hedge.

Shelby and Mackenzie — the uniformed Trail Guide Gals RJ had seen before — were pulling their cookie-filled wagon down the street.

"And the Doyles' is the yellow house," Shelby was saying.

"They only ordered one box," Mackenzie said, checking her order form.

RJ gestured to the wagon.

"And there they are," he said to Hammy. "America's most coveted cookies. Love Handles, Skinny Mints, Neener Neeners, and Smackeroons. And guess what? They're all *yours*!"

Hammy's mouth dropped open. "*Whooo!*" he gasped.

He started to slide down the tree towards the hedge . . . and the cookies.

RJ reached out and grabbed his tail.

"Whoa, whoa. Hold on there, fella. I love your energy, but you just can't take 'em."

Hammy blinked back tears. "But you said they're *mine*!"

RJ patted the little squirrel on the head. "They *will* be, if we successfully marry your manic energy to my brilliant plan. You with me, kid?"

Hammy scratched his head with his hind leg. "I . . . I . . . I . . . I . . ."

RJ grinned. "The I's have it! Let's ride."

Down below, on the other side of the hedge,

Shelby was looking at her order form. "I thought Mrs. Johansson was allergic to chocolate," she said.

"Really?" Mackenzie raised her eyebrows.

"Yeah," Shelby said. "If she eats it, her face, like explodes or something."

Mackenzie shook her head. "Whoa. That is, like, so unfair."

Shelby stared at the order form and made a face. "Really. How many boxes of Love Handles can one person eat?"

RJ and Hammy scampered behind a parked car, only a few feet away from the two Trail Guide Gals. The squirrel stopped short when he saw his face reflected in the car's bumper.

"Hey!" he hissed, shaking his finger at his reflection. "You stay away from those cookies. They're mine!"

RJ looked back at Hammy. Could he be that dim?

He tapped the car's bumper. "That's just your reflection," he explained.

Hammy frowned. "Well, whatever he is, he's not coming," he said. "I don't want him to."

RJ sighed. This was going to be a little harder than he had thought.

"We've got a lot of work to do," he said firmly,

steering Hammy away from the bumper. "C'mon, step into my office."

Hammy nodded.

"Now, listen up, kid," RJ went on. "What we're going for here is a vicious, man-eating rabid squirrel. Can you handle that?"

Hammy looked puzzled. He raised his hand.

"Uh, yes, Hammy?" RJ asked.

"I don't get it," Hammy said. "Rabbits aren't vicious. They're all cute and cuddly, so —"

RJ shook his head. "Ra-BID. Not rab-BIT."

Hammy nodded happily then looked confused. "Oh . . . what?"

RJ ignored him. "Okay, so first — we're gonna muss your fur." RJ messed up Hammy's fur from his head to the tip of his tail. "Ooh, that's looking good. Alright. Now, we're gonna mat the fur just a little bit . . . a little puff on the tail, stop it, puffier. *Mmm-hmm.* Liking that a lot."

Then he stepped back to admire his handiwork.

"Okay. Now, show me that wild look in your eye, Hammy."

Hammy made a goofy face. "I can burp my ABCs," he said. "A, B, C —"

RJ gritted his teeth. "Hammy, I just really need you to focus right now. Okay?"

"Okay," Hammy said gloomily.

"You just need something to make you look like you're having a fit . . . I know!" RJ reached into his golf bag.

"Let's see. Hang on a minute. Not that, not that, no, no . . ."

He tossed out the boomerang, a yo-yo, some golf balls, and a nail clipper. Ah . . . there it was! His can of whipped cream. He took it out and shook it. Then he sprayed the white foam around Hammy's mouth.

"NOW you look rabid!" he proclaimed.

The boomerang zoomed back, knocking Hammy over and out.

RJ rolled his eyes. This was going to be a LOT harder than he'd thought.

Verne stuck his head through the hedge and looked around.

"Hammy?" he called.

But Hammy was nowhere in sight.

Taking a deep breath, Verne pushed the rest of his body through the hedge.

What am I getting myself into? he thought. But he knew he had no choice.

He had to save Hammy from that insane raccoon before the poor little squirrel did something really foolish.

Down the street, RJ was pushing Hammy towards the two Trail Guide Gals.

"Now, come on," he hissed. "I'll be right behind you. Go on, get out there and act crazy!"

Hammy looked at RJ. He took a deep breath. Then he launched himself at the two girls.

"I am a crazy rabbit-squirrel!" he shrieked. *"I WANT MY COOKIES!!"*

Hammy ran wildly around the legs of the Trail Guide Gals. Shelby and Mackenzie looked down at the little squirrel in disbelief. Then they grabbed for their Guide Gals manual. There had to be something in it about squirrels behaving badly. . . .

"I'm *RABID*!" Hammy yelled. "I'm foaming at the mouth. I'm a foaming, very scary, rabbit-squirrel!"

Shelby and Mackenzie stared down at their manual. *"Rabies,"* it read. *"Symptoms: crazy eyes, foamy mouth, erratic behavior, chasing tail. . . ."*

"*RABIES!!!*" the two girls screamed.

Hammy's eyes lit up. He turned towards RJ, who was hiding behind a tree.

"It's working!" he said excitedly.

"Behind you!" RJ cried.

"I know!" Hammy said happily. "You're right behind me —!"

Behind him, Shelby raised the Trail Guide Gals manual. She then brought it down hard on Hammy's head.

"Take that!" she shouted.

"*Waaaaaa!*" Hammy shrieked.

Mackenzie pulled out a can of pepper spray and blasted Hammy full in the face.

"*No, no, no, no, no! Oh, no! Yaaaaaaa!*" Hammy squealed.

Just then, Verne came running up to RJ.

"What is going on?" he demanded. "Is that Hammy?"

"Everything is under control," RJ told him. "Just go back to the hedge."

Verne stared at RJ in disbelief. "You call that under control? Hammy's under attack!"

"He's working!" RJ protested.

But Verne was already gone. He had to save Hammy.

"I'm coming, Hammy!" he called.

"Verne! No! What are you doing?" RJ called after him. "Watch out!"

Verne stopped short in the middle of the street.

A giant street sweeper was headed right towards him.

As he froze in panic, the sweeper's giant brushes sucked him up and whirled him around and around. Then they shot him out again. He bounced off the street, popped out of his shell, and landed . . . on Shelby's face.

"*Ahhh!*" Verne screamed.

"*Ahhh!*" Shelby screamed. "Help me! Get it off of me!"

"Stay still!" Mackenzie commanded.

But Shelby was too freaked out to stay still. She whirled around in circles, dragging the terrified, naked turtle along with her.

Mackenzie whacked at the unprotected Verne with her manual. Just in time, Verne leapt off Shelby's face, and Mackenzie hit Shelby instead.

Verne dropped to the ground, his little green tail sticking up in the air. The two girls stared down at him for a second.

"Yuck! Gross! Eeeeew!" they yelped. Then they dropped everything and took off down the street.

Verne blinked and looked around.

RJ and Hammy rolled up to him with the captured red wagon, filled with Trail Guide Gals cookies.

"That was great!" RJ said enthusiastically, tossing Verne a cookie. "You, my friend, are a natural. Or should I say, '*au naturel*'?"

Verne looked down at himself. For the first time, he realized that he had no shell on.

"Huh? Oh." He blushed and used the cookie to cover himself up.

RJ turned to Hammy. "And you . . . you were awesome, my man! You had *me* scared. I was about to come out there and beat you with a book myself. You're alright, aren't ya? Of course you are. You are Hammy! Those bruises are gonna heal. You know what? Chicks dig scars!"

He started to pull the red wagon away. Hammy sat on top nibbling a cookie.

Verne started to get up when he heard voices. *Girls'* voices.

"There! There! It was over there! Right over there!"

Verne hid among some large rocks near the mailbox, where his shell had landed. He slipped into it just as the front door of the house behind him opened, and Shelby, Mackenzie, and their mother, Janis, came out and down the front walk.

They stopped next to him. He lay very still, pretending to be one of the rocks.

"That's where the squirrel attacked us!" Shelby said, pointing. "He had rabies or something. And there was this gross, naked amphibian thing. . . ."

"Reptile," Verne whispered under his breath.

"It's okay, girls," Janis said calmly. "Go inside, have a cookie, turn on the TV, and calm down."

"Thanks, Mom," Shelby said.

The two girls went back into the house. Janis reached down and picked up a crushed cookie box.

Gladys came walking over.

"I'm sorry, Janis," she said. "Did I just hear them say 'rabid squirrel'?"

Janis nodded. "I think they might just be overreacting."

Gladys frowned. "Well, I don't! I think we have a potential animal problem, and we need to nip it in the bud."

Janis started to back away. "Yeah, yeah, well, I have a casserole in the oven, gotta run."

"Fine," Gladys frowned. "You worry about your casserole and I'll worry about the invading vermin."

Gladys pulled out her cell phone and dialed a number.

"Yes," she said. "Do you sell animal traps?" She paused. "Humane ones? That won't hurt the animals? What good are those?"

SIX

Verne was walking back towards the hollow log when he saw something.

He stopped short.

It was a brightly colored, ripped-open box of Trail Guide Gals cookies.

Verne looked up. Ahead of him, a trail of torn cookie box wrappings were strewn all the way up to the hollow log. Near the log, the animals were cramming cookies into their mouths as if they were the last food on earth.

"*Mm-hm,*" RJ was saying. "That's right. Don't push. Plenty for everybody. Got a box right over here for you, Penny."

"Oh, jeepers, that is good!" Penny mumbled. "Kids, eat up. Anything that tastes this good has to be good for you."

"You feel that buzzing in the back of your skull?" RJ asked her.

"Yeah." Penny shoved another cookie in her mouth.

"That's called a sugar rush," RJ explained. "It's what keeps the humans from falling down."

He handed Penny a slightly dented can of soda. "You top that off with a little cola," he went on.

Hammy reached for a can.

RJ pulled it away.

"Whoa! Hold on, Hamsquad," he said, laughing. "The last thing *you* need is caffeine. You're revved-up enough already."

He turned to the others. "Stick with me, and we will have that wagon filled in no time!"

"Log," Verne corrected him.

RJ blinked. "What?"

"Log. Fill the log. You said wagon."

RJ recovered quickly. "Log, wagon — it's a common mistake. The important thing is — this is the beginning!"

The beginning, he thought gleefully. *They're falling for it! They're gonna help me gather Vincent's food! My life is . . . saved!*

The beginning . . . of what? Verne wondered,

staring at his friends as they gorged themselves on cookies.

This couldn't possibly be good. Could it?

Over the next few days, RJ led all the animals on a number of raids into the Rancho Camelot Estates.

The animals learned fast.

Stella and Heather emptied Gladys's trunk of food while she wasn't looking.

Penny and Lou used their quills to lift hot dogs right off a barbecue grill.

Stella popped out of the cake at a birthday party, sending all the kids running for cover. The animals then took all the food.

And it wasn't only food. RJ lifted a kid's backpack and found a portable video game player. He gave it to the porcupine kids, who spent endless hours playing wild car-chase games on it.

RJ also "found" an MP3 player and gave it to Heather.

The empty log was getting more and more full of food. There was almost enough in it to repay RJ's debt to Vincent.

Of course, once RJ took it all, there would be nothing left for the others to eat . . . .

But RJ didn't let that worry him. In fact, he didn't think about it at all.

Only Verne kept on looking for healthy, normal animal food. Slowly, he accumulated a pile of berries, nuts, and bark. He kept it at the back of the log.

But the others weren't interested. Chocolate marshmallow bars and crunchy Nutz 'n' Chocolate tasted so much better!

Verne was losing the battle, and he knew it.

Then two things happened.

One was something the animals didn't know about. Gladys made a call to an exterminator.

The other was much more dramatic. It began with a screech of tires. Then Verne heard someone cry out.

"Ozzie!" Verne gasped.

Frantically, he raced to the hedge and pushed his way through. An SUV with a blue cooler on top stood in the middle of the road, skid marks stretching out behind it.

In front of the SUV was a lifeless body . . . Ozzie's body.

Oh, no! Verne thought. *They've killed him! They've actually killed him!*

The humans in the car — a mom named Debbie and her two kids, Timmy and Skeeter — got out. They walked over to the small, furry form lying, helpless, in the middle of the street.

"Whoa, Mom!" Timmy said. "You hit a possum!"

"Oh, my goodness!" said Debbie.

"Do you think it's dead?" Skeeter wanted to know. "Can I poke it?"

"No!" Debbie said. She stared down at Ozzie. "The little dear. I feel terrible about this. These poor creatures . . ."

Verne hung his head in sorrow. *This was bound to happen*, he thought. *I knew it —*

Just then, RJ poked his nose out of a mailbox near the curb, just behind the SUV.

Then four other animals peeked out too.

RJ gave the signal and the animals crept towards the SUV.

Verne's mouth dropped open.

The animals scampered up to the roof and began to undo the straps that held the blue cooler in place. Then they started pushing it to the rear of the SUV.

Verne stared at them in confusion.

Just then, Gladys Sharp came out of her house. She moved towards Debbie and the kids.

"Debbie?" she said. "I don't remember seeing a permit for a gathering. Groups of more than one who wish to —"

She looked down and noticed Ozzie.

"Ewww!"

"Timmy?" Debbie turned to her older son. "Get the shovel from the car, please."

The animals on the roof froze. If Timmy came around to the back of the SUV, he would see them.

RJ stared down at Ozzie, willing the possum to do something . . . anything.

Ozzie twitched.

The humans jumped back.

"Hey, Mom! It's not dead!" Skeeter said.

Timmy turned around and rejoined the others. The animals all breathed a sigh of relief. They kept pushing the cooler towards the back of the SUV.

Ozzie, in the meantime, was acting his head off. This would be the greatest death scene a possum had ever played.

He struggled to his feet. The humans jumped back another step.

Then he staggered around, squeaking like mad.

"Mother, is that you?" he squeaked. "I see a tunnel . . . beckoning me into the light. Move towards the light."

Timmy stared in fascination.

"What do you think it's doing?" he asked his mom.

"Maybe we knocked his brains loose or something," Skeeter offered.

Verne stared, first in horror and then in disgust.

He headed for the back of the SUV.

"I'm telling you," he called to RJ. "You went too far this time. Let's just get out of here and leave this, this —"

The cooler had reached the end of the SUV. RJ tipped it over and it fell . . . right onto Verne.

"*Ooof!*" Verne said, flattened.

"Nice catch!" RJ said, scampering down to the ground.

"You're dangerous. You're insane!" Verne croaked from under the cooler.

On the other side of the SUV, Ozzie was finishing his performance. He sank to his knees.

"Sweet music, I'm going home!" he squeaked. "Goodbye, cruel world! *Oooh . . . oooh . . .* rosebud. . . ."

He fell on his back, his tongue dangling out.

"*Now* can I poke him?" Timmy wanted to know.

"*No!*" Debbie said.

Gladys shook her head. "You see? This is exactly why I called the exterminator, to kill them before they get hurt like this."

In the meantime, Verne had squirmed out from under the cooler.

"Everybody get out of here — right now!" he commanded.

"Right!" RJ said crisply. "Kids, grab those handles. Let's go. Pull out!"

The animals dragged the heavy cooler towards the hedge.

"Ow," Hammy said. "I threw out my back."

Suddenly, Verne felt the ground tremble. The rev of a large engine filled the air.

His tail began to tingle like mad. He hid under the SUV.

He looked behind him and stared under the SUV as a large pest control truck drove up.

On top of the truck was a statue of a man, holding a large hammer. The man was smashing the statue of a small sweet rabbit.

The license plate on the truck read, VERMIN8TR.

The door opened and out stepped Dwayne La Fontaine.

Dwayne was dressed in a jumpsuit. He wore thick glasses, and his thinning hair was plastered to his shiny skull.

As Verne watched in horror, Dwayne strapped on a utility belt crammed full of animal trapping devices.

Then he swaggered up to Gladys and the others.

"I believe," he said, "someone phoned about an animal problem? The solution is standing before you. Dwayne La Fontaine is here."

"Where have you been?" Gladys said, annoyed. "I'm throwing a 'Welcome to the Neighborhood' party tomorrow, and so far, Debbie's car has killed more animals than you have."

"Take it easy, ma'am." Dwayne smiled down at her. "I personally guarantee that there will not be a living thing at this party."

Verne stared at Dwayne. Then his head whipped around.

Unnoticed by the humans, the animals were still slowly dragging the cooler towards the hedge.

"Leave it! Leave it!" Verne hissed, racing over to them.

Dwayne walked over to Ozzie. He leaned over and took a large sniff.

"Now, what do we have here?" Dwayne sniffed again. "Didelphis marsupialis virginiana. Approximately ten pounds. Male."

"I . . . I think he's dead," Debbie explained.

"Oh, really?" Verne asked, staring at her. "Do you in fact have an associate's degree from Vermtech? I think he wants you to *think* that he's dead.

"What he's really in," Dwayne went on, "is what we in the trade call a 'voluntary shock state.'" He sniffed again. Then he listened. "Look at him closely. You can see him breathing."

Ozzie carefully opened one eye and looked over towards the hedge. RJ and the animals had almost made it.

RJ signaled to Ozzie. Ozzie winked.

"I certainly hope he's not in any pain," Gladys said piously.

Dwayne grabbed a claw-like device from his belt and reached towards Ozzie.

Ozzie leapt up and sprinted for the hedge.

"Ahhhh! Kill it! Kill it!" Gladys shrieked.

"You were a great audience!" Ozzie squeaked over his shoulder.

He and the others made it to the hedge just in time.

Only Verne was left outside. He cowered under the SUV as Dwayne moved towards it.

"Alright, what am I up against here?" Dwayne said to himself. He sniffed a few times. "Possum, porcupine, skunk, squirrel, raccoon . . . amphibian."

"Reptile," Verne said under his breath.

Dwayne took another sniff. "No. Make that reptile."

Dwayne looked under the SUV.

But Verne was gone.

Back in the clearing, Verne found the animals celebrating.

RJ high-fived Lou and low-fived the kids. Ozzie mopped his brow with a hankie.

"That's what I call a super-duper performance there, fella!" Lou said, slapping the possum on the back.

"I wanna do it again! I wanna do it again!" Hammy squealed, hopping around on one foot.

"*Beyond* super," RJ said, smiling at Ozzie. "They were riveted, man. You were awesome!"

Heather stepped forward. "Dad, I just gotta say. That was, uh, that was pretty good."

Ozzie beamed.

"Props for the Ozman!" Quillo yelled.

"Ozman! Yeah!" the other animals chorused.

Ozzie bowed graciously. Then he turned to RJ.

"But let's not forget our brilliant leader — RJ!"

The animals hooted and hollered their approval. They gathered around RJ. Hammy gave him a hug.

"That RJ sure knows what he's doing!"

"You're my hero there, fella."

Verne stared as RJ ate up all the affection. The raccoon was loving every minute of it.

Heather stepped forward. "RJ, come this way. We wanna show you something."

Heather led the way into a large, nearby willow tree.

Under the tree's drooping branches, the animals had assembled a new family room, complete with lounge chairs and TV. And in the corner, in a place of honor, was a comfy-looking car seat.

Hammy gestured to it. "Look . . . we've got a place for you right here," he told RJ.

RJ just stared. "That's . . . for me?" he finally asked.

"Yeah," Lou said proudly. "Is it anything like what you're used to there?"

RJ shook his head slowly. "This isn't anything like what I'm used to, Lou," he said quietly.

Hammy snapped open a soda can.

"Here," he said, handing the can to RJ. "I'm not supposed to drink this."

"Thanks," RJ said. He took a sip. Then he noticed a golf bag in the corner. "Is that my bag?" he asked.

"Yeah," said Heather shyly. "We brought it in here so you wouldn't have to sleep up in that old tree."

"Really?" said RJ. He blinked twice.

"And look, RJ. Check this out!" Bucky said. "We totally hooked up the TV."

"I hot-wired the HD converter," Quillo added.

"Prepare to see nose hairs," Spike said proudly.

Heather handed RJ the remote.

"Here," she said. "You take the remote before my dad does."

RJ took it, staring around.

"This is nice, guys — really nice," he said.

He turned on the TV.

"We now return to — 'The Scoundrel Among Us'!" an announcer's voice rang out.

"You should be ashamed of *yourself*," a woman in a long dress said to a man. "We let you into our family and you've deceived us . . ."

RJ quickly changed the channel. It sounded like they were talking about him.

A man was talking to a woman. "I gave you my heart and you ripped it into a million pieces!"

RJ guiltily changed the channel again.

"Get real, Kevin," a TV psychologist was telling a sniveling man. "'Cause when you feel like a dirt bag, it's because you ARE a dirt bag."

RJ turned the TV off.

Lou nodded. "Aw geez! He tells it like it is, doesn't he? Right, RJ? Right? Right?"

But RJ was gone.

"Whoa," RJ muttered to himself as he walked towards the food log. He was feeling extremely uncomfortable. They were being so nice, welcoming him into their family, and he was . . . he was a fraud and a fake. "What are you doing, man? You are getting in way too deep. Now, just get the food and feed the bear, get the food and feed the bear — *AHHHHH!*"

RJ stared into the log.

Just a few hours ago, it had been crammed with food.

Now, it was totally empty!!

RJ raced into the log, heart pounding. But there was nothing there.

Then he heard a familiar *squeak, squeak, squeak* in the distance. It was the *squeak, squeak, squeak* of a red wagon. And it came from the other side of the hedge.

"VERNE!!!!!!!" he screamed.

SEVEN

On the other side of the hedge, Verne was pulling the red wagon — a tower of food piled on top — across a grassy backyard.

RJ popped his head through the hedge. He stared around wildly. Then he saw the turtle struggling with the wagon.

"Verne!" he yelled. "What are you doing?" He raced over to the wagon and started to tug at it.

"I'm getting things back to the way they were," Verne said stubbornly.

"No, don't," RJ babbled. "How about I just leave?"

Verne stared at him. "Good. You leave, and I return this stuff to the rightful owners."

"What?" RJ gasped. "Why?"

"Because we've angered the humans," Verne said firmly.

He pointed.

The Vermin8tr truck was still parked in the street.

"Remember the sniffer guy?" Verne went on. "I'm giving this back so he won't *kill* us."

Verne tugged at the wagon. RJ tugged back.

"Verne, you don't understand!" RJ said desperately. "WE NEED THIS STUFF."

"No we don't." Verne kept tugging.

"YOU CAN'T TAKE IT!" RJ yelled.

"YES I CAN." Verne glared at the raccoon.

"Let go!" RJ insisted. "I have to have it!" He pulled hard on the wagon.

Verne pulled back. He stumbled over a root in the ground and fell. The wagon rolled over him and caught on something else in the ground. An anchor attached to a chain tumbled out of the dirt.

RJ stared at the chain.

Then he looked around. The ground around him was destroyed — dead, clawed grass and shrubs, holes dug everywhere.

RJ looked at the chain again. His eyes followed it across a stretch of ground.

It led to a doghouse with a sign over it that said NUGENT. Inside the doghouse was a large, ferocious-looking Rottweiler.

RJ froze.

"Verne," he whispered. "Move slow, keep your voice low, and follow me."

"What?" Verne got up and started to tug at the wagon again.

"Shhh!" RJ murmured.

"No," Verne said.

"Shhhhh!" RJ hissed urgently.

"No," Verne said clearly. "I'm not falling for any more of your smooth talk. I don't know what you're up to, but my entire shell is tingling. And you know what? I'm listening to it this time, and I'm putting my foot down."

Verne put his foot down — hard — onto a rubber dog toy.

SQUEAK!

Nugent woke up.

Play? his doggy brain thought.

He stepped out of the doghouse.

Verne stared in horror. He started to back away — and stepped on the dog toy again.

SQUEAK!

Then he stumbled against another dog toy.

HONK!

"Play! Play! Play! Play! Play!" Nugent barked happily.

Verne turned and started to run. The giant dog ran after him, his chain dragging behind him.

Before Verne knew what had hit him, Nugent had picked him up in his slobbering jaws and was whipping him back and forth.

Nugent happily slammed Verne into the red wagon. The tower of food trembled.

Behind a bush, RJ stared.

"*Ahhhhhhh!* This is horrible!" he gasped. "The *food*!"

RJ grabbed a nearby rag doll to use as a shield as he tried to creep up to the wagon. If he could just get there while the dog was distracted, he could roll the food away and back through the hedge —

"Let's play!" said the doll in a mechanical voice.

RJ skidded to a halt.

Nugent stopped chewing on Verne.

"Play!" he yelped, turning toward RJ and dropping Verne. The turtle crashed to the ground, landing on his stomach.

"*Ahhhh,*" he groaned.

Nugent bounded towards the doll and RJ. Verne tried to stumble away, but Nugent's chain grabbed him by the shell and dragged him along, too.

"Play! Play! Play! Play! Play! Play! Play!" Nugent barked.

"Down boy, sit, roll over!" RJ said frantically as he dodged to escape Nugent's dripping, slavering jaws.

"Play!" Nugent barked again.

"Play dead!" RJ screamed. But Nugent paid no attention. He just kept on coming.

As he closed in on RJ, the hook on the end of his chain grabbed hold of the handle of the red wagon. Verne slid off the chain and slammed into the pile of food on the wagon. He lay there, stunned. The wagon, with Verne on board, was being pulled behind Nugent as he raced across the backyard, happily pursuing RJ.

"Play! Play! Play! Play!" woofed Nugent.

"Atta boy, Verne, save the food!" RJ yelled. "I'll lose the dog!"

RJ ran towards the fence. Nugent ran after him, dragging the chain, wagon, food and turtle.

The chain caught on a lawnmower, which joined

the parade. Then the chain flipped the lawnmower's on/off switch on.

The blades swung into life.

Verne fell off the wagon onto the chain again, hanging above the whirring blades. Food slid off around him and was sliced into teeny, tiny bits by the sharp blades.

"You're dropping all the food, man!" RJ called to him.

RJ turned back to Nugent. "Are you hungry?" he said desperately. He pointed to a nearby neighbor, who was standing at his barbecue grill. "Look. Food!"

Nugent skidded to a halt. He turned and sniffed the air. Then he raced off towards the neighbor's yard, barking happily. He crashed headlong into the man at the barbecue. The chain wrapped around the barbecue's gas canister and pulled it free. The food on the grill went flying, covering the man with barbecue sauce.

The man screamed.

"That's right!" RJ called to Nugent. "Look! More people! Play with them!"

"Play, play, play, play, play!" Nugent barked.

His head whipped around. There *were* more people — sitting over there, on that patio!

Nugent ran up to them, crashing into patio furniture and sending a large umbrella flying into the air. The humans scattered like leaves. Nugent's chain wrapped around a lounge chair and the umbrella and tossed them onto the wagon.

As Nugent ran, sparks flew, igniting the gas canister, which was still attached to the chain.

Nugent — followed now by the red wagon (with Verne and the food on board), the lawn mower, a flaming gas canister, and the lounge chair — kept going.

"Verne! Unhook the chain!" RJ screamed.

Verne struggled to unhook the chain from the wagon, but it was no use.

Then Nugent's collar broke.

Verne slammed back into the pile of food in the wagon as Nugent bounded away. The wagon kept rolling forward. A can of potato chips went flying into the air.

"No!!!!" shrieked RJ, grabbing for the crisps. He caught them and hugged them to his chest.

"Yes," RJ said to the chips. "Bad chips."

Suddenly, he was caught up in the whipping chain, which was still attached to the wagon.

"Verne!" he yelled. "I told you to unhook the chain —"

The gas canister exploded, sending the wagon, the food, Verne, and RJ high into the sky, trailed by the lawnmower and lawn furniture.

"Oh, boy," Verne said.

The umbrella flew open. Verne grabbed it just as the wagon floated over an airplane and began to fall back to earth. RJ reached for the umbrella handle and caught it just in time, letting go of the chips can as he did.

Verne and RJ started to drift to the ground as the can popped open, raining chips all around them.

Below, Gladys had just come out of her house and was walking to her SUV. She was on her cell phone.

"Garbage cans are not to be on the curb before eight," she was saying when the empty can hit the car.

She looked up.

"AHHHHHHHHHH!"

A red wagon, connected to a lawnmower, a chair,

and a flaming gas canister, was headed towards her SUV.

She jumped out of the way just in time.

The wagon and the gas canister hit.

The SUV exploded.

The now-burning wagon launched into the sky, setting the umbrella on fire.

Verne and RJ blew on it desperately, but it was no use. In a second, the umbrella had burned to a crisp.

"You're the devil," Verne said calmly as he and RJ started to plummet toward the earth.

They landed with a crash on the other side of the hedge.

The wagon landed next to them.

So did several potato chips, fell neatly into a perfect stack.

RJ smiled.

The battered blue cooler, which had been on top of the exploded SUV, smashed into the wagon, destroying the stack of chips.

"Nooooo! Nooooooo!!!!" RJ groaned.

The other animals — who had been watching the scene in horror — ran up to help.

Lou reached them first. He stared at Verne, who was lying on his back.

"Verne? You alright there? Gimme a hand, Oz."

Ozzie and Lou began to turn Verne right-side up again.

"What the heck happened?" Penny asked.

"It's gone!" RJ sobbed. "The food . . . it's gone!"

Heather put her hand on RJ's shoulder.

"Gone?" Stella stared at RJ. "How's it gone?"

"Ask . . . *him*!" RJ said, pointing to the dazed Verne.

Everyone turned to the turtle.

"Verne?" Stella said.

"I returned it to its rightful owner," Verne said stiffly.

Lou and Ozzie, who had been holding Verne, dropped him. "What???" they chorused.

Everyone backed away from Verne.

"We, like, worked our tails off, you know," Heather began. "Like, a lot, and the food we gathered was totally . . . you know, and you're, you're all . . . whatever."

Ozzie shook his head. "Yeah, Verne. What were you thinking? The log was full!"

"Full of junk," Verne said, trying to roll over on his stomach.

"What are you saying there, that the, uh, food we gather *our* way isn't as good as the food we gather *your* way?" Lou stared at Verne accusingly.

"*Your* way???" Verne exploded. "You mean *his* way!!! You have got to trust me on this! Don't you understand there's something wrong with this guy? My tail tingles every time I get near him!"

Stella walked over to RJ.

"Oh," she said angrily. "So we're supposed to go hungry because your butt's vibrating? I'm startin' to think that little tingle of yours is just you bein' jealous."

"Jealous???" Verne plopped over onto his stomach and stood up. "Of *him*??? Can't you see that RJ is just using you? I mean, he's filling you full of false hope and telling you how wonderful you are —"

RJ stepped forward. "Somebody should, Verne. All *you* do is hold them back."

Verne stumbled over to RJ and stared at him. "You know what I hold them back from? *Extinction.* Because if they listen to half the stuff you're telling them, they'll be dead within a week. You are only interested in taking advantage of them because they are too stupid and naïve to know any better —"

Verne stopped himself suddenly and looked around. The others stood there, staring at him with stunned and hurt faces.

"I'm not stupid," Hammy said in a tiny voice.

Lou frowned. Penny glared at Verne as she scooped up her three kids.

"Okay," Verne said quickly. "I didn't mean . . . uh, I meant ignorant."

The others kept staring.

"Uh, to the ways . . . over there," Verne stumbled on.

The animals glared at Verne for another moment. Hammy's lower lip trembled.

Then they all turned and slowly trudged away.

Verne started after them. "Come on, you guys. You know I didn't mean it like that. Don't do this . . . Stella, Ozzie . . . Hammy, you know I didn't . . . Hammy . . ."

"I'm not stupid," Hammy repeated sadly, walking away.

Stella put her arm around him. "Come on, Hammy," she said gently.

"Please . . ." Verne said.

But they were gone.

EIGHT

Verne wandered into the willow tree.

There was RJ's chair. Next to it were some photos of RJ and the other animals, smiling happily.

All except Verne. He was scowling.

Verne sighed and left. He walked towards the hedge.

A bag of chips was lying nearby. Verne glanced at it. Then he walked on.

He picked up a berry as he wandered over to the creek.

He looked down at the water, staring at his reflection.

He dropped the berry in. His reflection broke up into a thousand little pieces.

It looked just like he felt . . . all broken up inside.

He stared at the water for a little while longer. Then he walked away.

He walked for a long, long time, hating himself for what he'd said. His family would probably never forgive him. They *shouldn't* forgive him. What he had said was unforgivable.

Back at the willow tree, RJ was saying goodnight to his new family. He looked down at the sleeping animals and then up at the sky.

Stars twinkled in the sky. The moon was nearly full.

As he watched, the constellation Ursa Major — the big bear — turned into Vincent. The moon became a frightened raccoon.

"Moon's full, RJ." RJ could hear Vincent's voice in his head. "See you in the morning."

The starry bear opened its cavernous jaws and took a huge bite out of the raccoon moon.

RJ gulped.

"Alright," he said to himself. "Let's get back on track. You've got a red wagon and a blue cooler. Nobody said they had to be pretty. All you need to do to save your life is to get the food. No problem."

RJ heard something and stopped.

He zipped over to the hedge and cautiously peered out the other side.

"Hah!" Dwayne laughed. "This'll cut you down to size."

He hit a switch.

Sharp, gleaming spikes shot out of the sprinkler holes all over the lawn.

"I got ya!" Dwayne said gleefully.

RJ pulled back, his hand at his throat. He gulped.

Dwayne walked over to the path and put a lamp down.

"I'm just walking here on the lawn," Dwayne said, doing just that. Then he stopped and looked back at the lamp. "I didn't notice a little bunny was right there. . . ."

He picked up a stick and poked the lamp.

Claws shot out of the lamp and clamped shut with an ominous *clang*.

RJ stared.

Dwayne moved around the lawn, setting off traps.

Clang, clang, clang.

"You're done, aren't you?" he said as a flamingo lawn ornament chewed up a dog toy.

"Taste the steel," he added, watching a garden gnome devour a pink rubber ball.

"Splitting headache, huh?" he giggled as another trap sprang shut around a small toy. "Say good-bye to your heartbeat!"

RJ's mouth was dry. He started to tremble.

"You!!"

RJ jumped three feet.

The voice belonged to Gladys. Luckily, she was talking to Dwayne.

Dwayne turned and walked back towards the house. Gladys was standing on the patio.

RJ quickly climbed a tree to get a better look.

"I trust," Gladys said, pointing to a nasty-looking contraption, "you installed this one? The Depelter Turbo?"

"*Officially? No, ma'am,*" Dwayne said cautiously. Then he leaned towards Gladys. "This baby," Dwayne explained in a stage whisper, "is illegal in forty-eight states."

Gladys glared at him. "My perennials have been trampled, my garden violated, and my SUV exploded.

I don't care if this thing's against the Geneva Convention. I want it."

Dwayne's teeth gleamed. "Well if I *had*, it would work a lot like this. . . ."

He reached over and flicked a switch near the front door.

Ten lasers switched on.

Then he tossed a small stuffed rabbit out into the yard.

It crossed one of the laser beams.

Searchlights turned on. A siren screamed.

RJ held his ears.

A second later, a smoking stuffed bunny skin landed right in front of him.

In the morning, RJ looked at the list of goodies he needed to collect if he were going to save himself from Vincent.

"I am so dead," he said.

He wadded up the list and tossed it away.

"Hey, RJ?" Verne suddenly called. "I need to talk to you"

RJ jumped.

"Because it's time to face the truth." Verne

continued. RJ slumped onto his golf bag. Verne sat down next to him.

"I'm slow to accept change," Verne began. "I mean, it's true that everything about you makes my tail tingle like never before . . . but maybe it's wrong and they're right. Maybe I'm just . . . jealous."

"*You* should not be jealous of *me*, okay?" RJ said. "You've got a good thing here. Those guys are . . . well, they're pretty great, you know."

"Of course I know, which is why I have to make it up to them," Verne said. "I need to get all that food back."

"You and me both, pal. But that's not gonna happen." RJ said, shaking his head.

"Why not?" Verne asked. "You did it in a week, you can do it again."

"I don't have a week, Verne." RJ said. This was it, the moment of truth. He picked up the crumpled list and smoothed it out, showing it to Verne. "There's something I need to tell you . . . about this . . ."

Beep. Beep.

RJ looked up. What was that? He scampered up a nearby tree to look. A grocery delivery truck was backing into Gladys' driveway.

"Yes! Yes, yes, yes!" RJ almost shouted. He was back in business.

"What is this?" Verne asked, climbing the tree to join him.

Seeing the list in Verne's hand, RJ had to think fast.

"Um, that's a list that I made of all the stuff you lost. But I know a place so full of food, we could get it all back in one night."

"Where?" Verne asked in confusion.

"Inside that house," RJ said, pointing down at Gladys' house.

A stunned Verne slid out of his shell and fell out of the tree.

"Man," RJ said, tapping the shell. "What is the point of this thing?"

"Just send it down, okay?" Verne covered himself with a leaf.

In the clearing, Verne faced his friends. He stared at them, but didn't speak. The animals stared back at him, shifting uncomfortably.

". . . and you know, words were said, feelings were hurt, squirrels got angry . . ."

Hammy looked like he might cry.

"But what Verne is trying to say is . . . ," RJ continued.

"I'm sorry." Verne blurted out.

The animals looked at Verne. Then Hammy, dear, sweet Hammy opened his arms.

"Come here," he said.

All the animals joined in a group hug.

That evening, RJ pointed at a three-dimensional model of the hedge, Gladys's backyard, and Gladys's house. The other animals stood around, watching closely.

"Now, the traps are set here." RJ pointed with his gold club. "Here — here — here — here — here — here — here — here — here — here. Big one here — here — here — here — and maybe a few over here."

"Gee," Stella said drily. "Is that all?"

"No," RJ shook his head. "There's a bunch of red lights all over *here*. Okay. This is us."

He reached into his bag, pulled out a bunch of Monopoly game pieces and dumped them beside some sprigs of rosemary, which were standing in for the hedge.

"Can I be the car?" Hammy said hopefully.

"I wanna be the car!" Bucky shouted.

"Spike is the car," Spike said firmly. "You be the shoe."

"The shoe is lame," Bucky snorted.

"Why don't you be that snazzy iron over there?" Lou suggested.

RJ held up his paws. "Hey! It's not important! Besides . . . *I'm* the car. I'm *always* the car." He pointed to the car. "Now, the plan works in three simple steps. Step one: kill the lights. Step two: get inside. Step three: get out with mountains of food."

Ozzie stared at the model. "But this place is like a fortress. Walls, so high. Doors, impenetrable. How will we get in?"

RJ reached into his bag again and pulled out a cell phone. He clicked it on and showed the animals a short film of the cat entering the cat door.

"The collar is the key," he explained. "Literally. The collar — it's like a key — that opens the door — and if —"

Stella snorted. "If what? You think that cat is just gonna hand over his collar to you?"

"Not to me, my femme fatale," RJ said, staring at Stella. "To *you.*"

"Me??!" Stella blinked.

"*You*, Stella," RJ told her, "will get that cat to *give you* his collar by using . . ."

"My stink." Stella sighed.

"No." RJ's eyes gleamed. "Your feminine charms."

Hammy burst into laughter. "*Ha-ha-ha!* Her feminine charms???"

The others stared at him. He clapped his paws over his mouth.

"Was that out loud?" he asked innocently.

Stella frowned. "Look, raccoon. Maybe that mask you're wearing is obstructing your view, but if you haven't noticed . . . I'm a *skunk*."

"On the outside, maybe," RJ said confidently. "But I'm lookin' *inside*, Stella, and I see a *fox*. And all we gotta do is get her out."

"Scissors."

RJ held out his paw, and Lou slapped a large set of pruning shears into his paw.

The animals were all gathered in a huddle around Stella.

"Scissors?" she said. "Whoa, hey, hey, hey, watch the —"

The air above her filled with a cloud of black and white hairs.

"Charcoal!" Penny called.

"Charcoal?" Stella yelped.

Hammy handed a bucket of black charcoal to Penny. Penny dumped the charcoal on Stella. Stella started to cough.

"Air freshener," RJ called.

Heather ran to him with a can of air freshener. He sprayed.

"Tomato juice."

"Tomato juice," Ozzie echoed, handing him a bottle.

"Cork."

"Cork?" Stella's voice rose to a shriek. "Don't you dare!!!"

"Just let me —" RJ said, ignoring her. "There!"

"Ow!" Stella squealed.

RJ threw his paws up in the air. "Whoa, stop! That's it. Ladies and gentlemen — our work here is done."

The animals all stepped back. Hammy gasped.

Stella was gorgeous. Her white stripe was gone, and she looked sleek and black and totally feline.

"Oh, my," gasped Lou.

"Jeepers," said Penny.

"She's all like . . . wow," marveled Heather.

RJ held up a shiny CD mirror so Stella could see herself in it.

She stared for a moment, then raised an eyebrow. "What — oh. Meow."

Verne just stared. It was amazing. It was incredible.

It just might . . . work.

NINE

Dwayne drove his truck through the neighbor-hood, on the lookout for predators.

A pink lawn flamingo loomed out of the dark-ness. Dwayne aimed a bolo launcher at it.

The bolo sliced the flamingo's head off.

"Oh, dang it," Dwayne muttered. "Those things are so lifelike."

Dwayne kept driving.

Nearby, RJ was in a tree, holding a fishing pole.

He swung the pole and launched the line into the air. It snaked past the laser beams in Gladys Sharp's backyard and caught on to the drainpipe on the roof of her house.

"Okay, Hammy," RJ said under his breath. "Go-go-go-go-go-go!"

Hammy slithered across the fishing line. His tail

almost set off the alarm . . . but he made it safely to the rooftop.

He jumped into the gutter, detached the hook, and sent the line back to RJ. Then he started to walk across the roof, stopping for a moment to pick up a cookie.

"No, no, no!" RJ whispered. "Hammy! I told you — that cookie's junk!"

"But I like a cookie," Hammy whined. He held it up and waved it at RJ.

"What's going on?" Verne called from down below. "Is everything okay?"

RJ gave Verne a thumbs-up. Then he reached into his bag and pulled out a laser pen.

He pointed the red dot onto the roof and then began tracing a line down the side of the house. Hammy followed it carefully, skirting the Depelter lasers.

"Come on, Hammy," RJ muttered to himself as Hammy made his way onto the lawn. "Follow the pretty light. There it is, that's it. That's it. Go get it. Uh-huh, that's it, that's it. Go get it, you little nut. Bingo!"

RJ led Hammy all the way to the Depelter Turbo ON/OFF switch.

Hammy turned it off.

RJ gave Verne another thumbs-up sign.

"Right," RJ muttered. "Step two."

A few minutes later, the red wagon — with everyone on board — flew into the backyard.

"Okay, gorgeous." RJ turned to Stella. "You're on."

Stella stepped out of the wagon and walked across the backyard. The rest of the animals took up their positions.

"Man." Stella rolled her eyes. "This had better be one stupid cat."

She sauntered up to the patio. Through the window, she could see the cat. He was curled up on a chair.

RJ turned to Hammy, who was holding a toy — the kind that made animal noises.

"Audio — go!" RJ whispered.

Hammy pulled the cord on the toy.

Mooooo!

Stella whipped around.

RJ grabbed for the toy. "Not cow, cat!" he hissed. "Gimme that!"

Verne groaned. "Maybe the cat likes a cow. Let's hope the cat likes a cow."

Inside the house, the cat opened his eyes and raised his head. Something was in the backyard.

He stretched lazily and hopped off the couch. Then he sauntered through the cat door and looked around.

"Who goes there?" he asked.

Stella gulped.

"You're a cat, you're a cat!" RJ whispered to Stella from behind some bushes.

"You're a cat," Stella said nervously. "That is, I'm a cat. I'm a cat. Uh . . . meow?"

She smiled alluringly.

The cat waved a paw dismissively. "Yeah. Right. Shoo. Go on, get away from here. My owner does not give scraps to common strays."

Stella blinked. "Common strays?! Alright, I'm done!"

She turned to leave.

From the bushes, RJ hissed at her. "Get the collar!"

Stella turned back quickly and plastered on a big smile.

"Gee," she said, sidling up to the cat. "That's a nice collar you got on. Mind if I have a look?"

"No, no, no!" the cat meowed. "Come no closer!

I must not be so near a creature of the outdoor woods." He sneezed. "Away with your filth!"

"My filth? *MY FILTH?*" Stella's eyes narrowed.

"Aw, jeepers," Penny groaned from the bushes. "Here we go."

Stella glared at the cat. "Okay, that's it. I am sick and tired of everybody taking one look at me and running away cause they think I'm filthy. Well, I've got news for you. I didn't get all primped and preened to have some overfed, pompous, puffball tell me he's too good for me. I got makeup on my butt, dude!"

"Stop!" The cat held up a paw. "No one has *ever* spoken to me like that." He paused, and then smiled. "It is bold. I like it."

Stella batted her eyes. "Well, believe me, there's more where that came from, puffball."

Behind the bushes, RJ let out his breath in a whoosh. Then he turned to the others.

"Alright, team. Let's boogie!"

The animals scooted towards the back door.

In the meantime, the cat was sniffing around Stella.

"You are strong," he murmured. "Your essence is . . . overpowering."

Stella glared at him. "What do you mean by that?" she said.

"It is . . . your eyes," the cat purred.

"My . . . eyes?"

"They are . . . luminous."

"Luminous?" Stella blushed. "Dang."

The other animals huddled around the cat door.

"I kinda bought this when you drew it in the dirt," Verne said to RJ, staring at the door. "But now that we're standing here . . . it is not gonna work."

He raised his hand. The cat collar landed on it. *Beep*. The cat door opened.

"Of course, I could be wrong," he added.

RJ peered inside the house. The coast was clear. He motioned to the animals to go inside.

Meanwhile, Stella stood outside with the cat, blocking his view of the door.

"So," she purred. "You got a name?"

"Yes," the cat replied. "It is a Persian name, for I am Persian. I was born Prince Tigeriess Mahmood Shabaz."

"Ooh, that's a mouthful," Stella said. "Can I just call you Tiger?"

Inside the house, the animals found themselves in the kitchen. They looked around, stunned.

"Wow."

"Jeepers."

"Awesome."

RJ went over to the refrigerator and opened it. Rows and rows of food gleamed out at them.

"Jeepers!" gasped Penny again.

RJ danced around the open fridge door. "Whoa! Animals are in the house!"

He reached over and kissed Verne. Then he went to work.

"Okay," he commanded. "Stations, everybody. Kids . . . security detail. Get that camera in position. Go! Go! Go!"

"We've got it!" said Spike, saluting. The porcupine kids scampered away.

"Hammy . . . load that wagon. Fast and furious."

"OK, RJ," said Hammy. "I'm on the QT!"

He zipped off.

RJ turned. "Penny, Lou — hit that fridge. Clean it out. Ozzie, Heather — cabinets and pantry. Clear the shelves."

"Everybody, let's move," Verne chimed in.

Hammy slid across the floor with an armful of food. "No grip. No grip," he cried, dropping a large jar of cookies with a crash.

RJ grabbed Hammy. "Less claw, more pad," he instructed.

Hammy nodded.

RJ beamed as he watched the red wagon filling up with food. "*Yes*," he thought, pumping his paw into the air. "*I'm gonna make it!*"

Upstairs, Quillo and Spike were placing the camera so that it would show Gladys, who was sleeping soundly, on the living room TV. Then they started to connect the wires that would send a picture of Gladys downstairs, where the animals could keep an eye on her.

In the living room, Bucky hopped up onto the coffee table and grabbed the remote. He turned the TV on, expecting to see Gladys sleeping.

Instead, the room filled with noise.

Outside, Tiger turned towards the house.

"What was that?" he asked.

"Uh —" Stella thought fast. "It was just the sound of my heart! Can't you hear it?"

She grabbed Tiger's head and crushed it up against her chest.

Back inside, Spike and Quillo finally finished wiring the camera. An image of Gladys appeared on the TV downstairs. Bucky breathed a sigh of relief and waved to RJ, who was peering out of the kitchen.

RJ nodded. "Okay, we're good," he said, turning to the others. "Go back to work."

The other animals had formed a food-passing chain. Ozzie passed to Penny, who passed to RJ, who passed to Heather, who then threw the food to Verne. Verne was supposed to put the food on a plastic wrap ramp that the animals had constructed from the kitchen to the cat door.

Hammy raced in and out of the door, grabbing food and putting it into the wagon.

RJ looked over the food as it flew down the plastic wrap ramp, searching for something.

"Chips, chips," he muttered.

But there were no potato chips to be seen.

Stella, still blocking Tiger's view of the back door, watched the wagon fill out of the corner of her eye.

"Inside," Tiger meowed, "I have many squeaky

toys and a most excellent climby thing. Come. We go."

He turned and moved towards the wagon.

"No!" Stella put a paw on his shoulder.

"I haven't told you about *me*," she said alluringly.

Back in the kitchen, RJ was busy searching the cupboards.

"Chips, chips, chips," he muttered, opening cabinet after cabinet.

A beeper on the coffee maker went off. The aroma of brewing coffee filled the air.

"What is that?" Verne asked.

RJ sniffed. "That's what gets humans out of bed in the morning."

The porcupine kids looked back over at the TV screen.

Gladys was no longer in her bed.

"Where'd she go?" asked Bucky.

That's when Gladys's foot appeared on the stairs.

Verne waved wildly at the porcupine kids. "Get down and stay down!" he hissed.

The three young porcupines pulled the TV manual over themselves and stopped breathing.

"Move! Move!" Verne called to the others.

The animals hid behind the kitchen island as Gladys entered the kitchen, yawning.

She picked up a cup and poured herself a cup of coffee.

Then she opened a high cabinet to get some creamer.

Inside the cabinet was a can of Spuddies potato chips.

Gladys closed the cabinet, turned, and left the kitchen. She started to climb the stairs.

"C'mon!" Verne hissed. "We've gotta go before she gets back!"

"No!" RJ held up a paw. "Not without the chips!"

He turned towards the cupboard. "Lou, Penny — back to the TV. Heather, keep an eye on that human."

"I'm on it, RJ," Heather said.

She raced for the stairs.

"No, Heather. Wait!" Ozzie rushed after her.

RJ started to climb up towards the can of potato chips.

"RJ!" Verne hissed. "The wagon's full. Let's get out of here!"

"Hang on, Vincent," RJ said. "This'll only take a second —"

"Vincent?" Verne stared at RJ.

RJ freaked. "WHERE!" he shrieked.

Verne frowned. "Who's Vincent?"

RJ bit his tongue. "Oh, Verne, Vincent — simple slip of the bear — TONGUE! Er, just bear . . . with me is what I meant to say, heh-heh. There's no bear —"

Verne's tail started to tingle like mad. But it was too late.

As Heather reached the top of the stairs, Gladys turned and saw her.

"*AHHHHHHH!*" Gladys screamed.

Heather quickly "played dead."

But Gladys kicked her.

Heather tumbled down the stairs. She landed at the bottom with a sickening thud. She lay still.

"Heather!" Ozzie screamed, racing towards her.

Gladys ran back into her bedroom to call Dwayne.

Ozzie reached Heather's side and shook her. "Oh, Heather!" he moaned.

Heather opened one eye.

"I thought you were dead."

Hugely relieved, Ozzie grabbed his daughter and gave her a big hug.

Heather smiled shakily. "I learned from the best, Dad," she said.

In the kitchen, RJ was still straining to reach the potato chips. "Come to Papa," he murmured.

Verne, climbing up after him, grabbed his tail and yanked him back down.

"What's going on, RJ?" he demanded.

"Nothing!" RJ insisted, turning to reach for the can again.

"Well then, let's get out of here," Verne said. "We have what we need."

"No we don't!" RJ shouted.

"What are you talking about?" Verne said. "We have more than enough!"

"HEY, LISTEN!" RJ shrieked. "I've got about THIS LONG to hand over that wagon-load of food to a homicidal bear, and if these chips aren't on the menu, then I will be!"

"What?" Verne blinked.

"LET . . . GO!" screamed RJ, grabbing for the can.

The can teetered on the edge of the shelf and then

fell, hitting the counter and sending the chips exploding everywhere.

Still on the phone, Gladys raced down the stairs and into the kitchen.

"*AHHHHHHHH!*" she shrieked again.

Outside, hearing the commotion, Stella moved away from Tiger.

"I'm sorry," she said. "It's just not going to work."

"Stella, Stella," Tiger cried. "Where are you going? STELLLLLAAAAA!!!"

Stella ignored him and raced for the cat door. As she squeezed through, the soot on her tail brushed off, revealing her for the skunk she was.

Inside, Gladys was chasing animals around, waving her broom.

RJ was desperately scooping up chips and shoving them into the can.

Stella moved forward. Behind her, Tiger entered the room. He grabbed her.

"Stella!" he said despairingly.

She turned to face him. "Look, Tiger. It's not you. It's because I'm a . . . I'm a . . ."

Gladys whirled around and caught sight of Stella.

"SKUUUUUUNK!" she screamed.

"Yeah, that." Stella nodded. "Sorry you have to see this —"

With a flourish, Stella lifted her tail.

"Fire in the hole!" she proclaimed.

WHOOOOOSH!

Gladys grabbed her nose. Her eyes watered, and she started to cough.

Outside, the Vermin8tr truck screeched to a halt. Dwayne got out and moved towards the door.

He sniffed.

Skunk, he thought.

Inside, Tiger was staring dreamily at Stella.

"The smell doesn't bother you?" she asked him, astonished.

"No," said Tiger. "I have terrible allergies. I can't smell a thing."

Stella's eyes lit up. "You . . . can't smell?"

She smiled.

RJ ran out the cat door, clutching the chip can in his paw.

Verne saw that RJ had abandoned them and knew it was up to him to save his family. He pointed towards the cat door. "To the hedge!" he yelled. "Go! Go! Go!"

The animals ran for the door. But Gladys reached it first and blocked it.

"Run! The other way!" Verne called.

The animals ran the other way. But as they did, the door opened and Dwayne appeared, wearing a gas mask and holding a net gun.

"*AHHH!*" screamed the animals.

"Let's party," Dwayne said, grinning.

He pointed the gun and fired.

The net wrapped around Gladys's bunny slippers. Gladys fell to the floor with a crash.

Dwayne pulled in the net and turned. Then he aimed the gun at Stella.

Tiger pushed Stella out of the way just in time. The net fell around him instead.

"Flee, my love," the cat commanded. Stella looked at him gratefully.

The animals turned to escape, screaming at one another.

"Dad, run!"

"Move, kids!"

"Run away!"

Verne looked around desperately. There — an open door that led —

"Come on, that way!" Verne shouted, pointing. "Outside!"

The animals launched themselves at the door. But the door was glass . . . and it was shut.

They slammed into it and slid down to the floor, dazed.

Dwayne came up just behind them.

"*Buenos días*, reptile," he said, smirking.

The net came down, trapping them all.

All except RJ, who had already rolled the red wagon, piled high with food, back through the hedge.

TEN

An hour later, the animals were stacked in cages outside Dwayne's truck.

"You've just been verminated!" Dwayne said, smiling evilly.

Gladys came out of the house and down the steps. Dwayne wrinkled his nose.

"Whoa, you stink!" he said.

Gladys started to sob. "That's because you let them into my . . . my . . . hou-hou-hou-house!"

Dwayne walked over to the truck and opened the back doors. "Hey, Nancy, stop your honkin'!" he said. "These little guys will be disposed of quickly and humanely."

Gladys glared at him. "No! Not humanely! As IN-humanely as possible!"

Dwayne started to load the animals into the truck.

"It was a pleasure doing business with you, ma'am," he said.

From inside his cage, Bucky started to whimper.

"What's he gonna do to us, Mama?" he asked.

"I don't know, baby," Penny said.

"I don't wanna die, Dad," Heather sniffed. "Not for real."

"There, there, sweetheart," Ozzie comforted her. "We'll be okay."

"Gee, Verne," Lou said. "You were right about that RJ. We shoulda listened. Sorry, there."

Verne stared over at the cliff face. He could see RJ, a small speck in the distance, wheeling the wagon of food towards Vincent's cave.

"No," Verne said, shaking his head. "I knew we couldn't trust him, and I got us into this. I should've known better."

Up on the cliff, RJ headed for the cave.

"Wow," a voice said.

"Vincent?" RJ gulped.

Vincent stepped out from behind a tree. He was holding a pair of binoculars.

"So I was on my way down there to kill you," he

began. He gestured down the cliff towards the Rancho Camelot Estates with the binoculars. "But I stopped to watch the show, and I gotta say . . . that right there is a thing of beauty."

He held up the binoculars and gestured for RJ to look.

RJ peered through them . . . and saw the animals in their cages, being loaded onto Dwayne's truck.

Dwayne threw the last cage into the truck and slammed the door.

RJ gasped.

Vincent pulled the binoculars away and shook his shaggy head. "That is the most vicious, deceitful, self-serving thing I've ever seen," he said admiringly. "I'm impressed. You take the food . . . and they take the fall. You keep this up, you're gonna end up just like me. Having everything you ever wanted."

RJ stared in horror as Dwayne's truck started to roll. It picked up speed and headed for the ramp to the freeway.

He hung his head in shame.

"But I already *had* that," he whispered, thinking about his car seat in the willow tree.

Vincent snorted. "What? *Them?* Who are you kidding? You're a scavenger, RJ, you always will be.

And that's a *good* thing. It's how we survive. So a few saps get hurt in the process . . ." He shrugged. "Tough. That's life. Trust me, you don't need them."

RJ looked up and stared at Vincent.

"Actually," he said quietly, "I do. And right now . . . they *really* need me. So I really . . . need this."

RJ grabbed the handle of the red wagon, hopped on board, and started to fly down the hill.

"RJ!!!!" Vincent hollered, taking off after him.

RJ rode the wagon down onto the highway. It zoomed across the divider and headed for the truck.

In the truck, Dwayne suddenly saw a red wagon piled high with food zooming straight towards him.

"*AHHHHH!*" he screamed.

The wagon hit the truck with a crash. RJ flew up into the air and landed on the hood.

"What the —" Dwayne yelled.

He jammed on the brake. The animal cages slammed towards the front of the van, smacking him in the back of the head.

He collapsed, unconscious.

With no driver, the van swerved around violently

from side to side. RJ hung on to the grille for dear life. The animals were flung around their cages and against the doors. One by one, the cage doors snapped open.

Finally, the van came to a stop.

Hammy whimpered. "I hurt my back again."

Ozzie peered around. "Heather? Are you okay?"

In the meantime, RJ scampered over the hood and peered in the window to make sure everyone was okay.

Verne stared out the window, blinking. *RJ. He came back for us,* Verne realized.

Stella saw RJ, too. She held up her fist angrily.

"You sorry sack of —" she began.

RJ held up his paws. "Whoa — Stella. This is a rescue. I'm rescuing you!"

But Stella couldn't hear him from inside the car. "I'm gonna gas you so hard, your grandchildren'll stink!" she shrieked.

Behind RJ, Vincent appeared, galloping towards the truck.

Verne saw him first.

"Bear!" Verne yelled, climbing onto the dashboard.

RJ frowned and pointed to his ears. He couldn't hear what Verne was saying.

"Bear!" Verne pointed again.

"Hair?" RJ asked, putting his ear up to the glass. "Dare?"

RJ suddenly blinked. He could see Vincent reflected in the glass.

"Oh," he said. *"BEAR!!!!"*

RJ leapt out of the way just as Vincent jumped onto the hood of the truck. The impact sent Verne flying back off the dashboard. He rammed into Dwayne's knee, which jammed Dwayne's foot against the gas pedal.

The truck lurched forward again.

The animals were thrown to the back of the truck as Vincent struggled to hold on to the hood.

He couldn't. As the truck picked up speed, he slid down onto the front grille.

"Whoa! Wha —" Vincent yelped.

RJ clung to the side mirror with all his strength. The steering wheel spun free, sending the truck careening all over the road.

"Whaaaah!" he shrieked.

Verne clambered up and grabbed the steering wheel, spinning it wildly.

"We're out of control!" he cried.

"We'll drive," said Spike.

"It's just like our video game!" Quillo added, joining him.

They jumped on the wheel, sending the van spinning around.

RJ was still hanging on to the side-view mirror, but what he saw in the mirror almost made him lose his grip — Vincent was *still* there.

"Verne, let me in!!" RJ yelled. He glanced over his shoulder again and darted away, just as a massive bear head filled the side window.

"RRROARRR!"

The noise frightened Verne and he fell onto the navigation system.

"Please select destination," a calm voice said.

"Take us home!" Hammy yelled. "Take us to the log!"

Hammy jumped onto the Navistar screen. Miraculously, he pressed the correct button.

"Return home selected," the voice said. "Make a legal u-turn."

"We got it!" Bucky shouted as he and the other porcupine kids began to spin the wheel.

Outside, RJ was in big trouble!

"Get back here!" Vincent roared, chasing the raccoon across the hood and around the van.

"Hammy!" RJ screamed as he passed the window again. "Let me in!"

"Not listening to RJ," Hammy said, holding his ears. "Not listening. Not listening. La la la la la . . ."

"Kids, lose that bear!" Verne ordered.

"What weapons do we have?" Bucky asked.

"We've got a hammer!" Spike said, pointing to a button that showed a man hitting a bunny with a hammer. It was the model on top of the truck. Spike pressed the button, and the hammer attached to the statue of the man on the roof swung around and hit Vincent. He roared.

Then he grabbed for the hammer. It ripped free.

He swung it at RJ, narrowly missing him. It crashed through the side window instead.

RJ took this as a sign and jumped into the van, crawling over the others for all he was worth. But he crawled too far and before he knew it, he was back outside with only an angry bear for company.

RJ tried to climb back in, but Ozzie was frantically rolling up the window.

"Let me in, let me in!!" RJ begged.

"No! Ring-tailed charlatan!"

Verne turned and saw RJ hanging on for dear life to the top of the window.

"He's trying to help us, just let him in!" Verne shouted at Ozzie.

"After what he did to us?" Stella gasped.

"But he came back!" Verne said.

Vincent growled as he chased RJ around the truck.

"And he brought a bear!" Lou pointed out.

At this all the animals started shouting at each other, until the porcupine kids decided to put a stop to things.

"Hey! No fighting while we're driving!" Spike said.

"We will turn this van around, mister!" Quillo added.

The other animals quieted down.

"He started it," Lou said sulkily, pointing at Verne.

"I'm telling you, he's just trying to help, really!" Verne said worriedly.

"But, Verne, you're the one who always says trust your tail," Ozzie said.

"But it's not tingling!" Verne said.

"Oh," the animals chorused.

"Why didn't you say so?" Stella asked.

"Hey!" RJ screamed from outside.

Ozzie rolled down the window, and RJ fell inside.

Vincent was back on the roof of the truck. This time, he sank his claws into the metal and started to peel it off like the top of a sardine can.

"You're dead, RJ!" he screamed. "And your friends are next!"

He reached for RJ, but he missed.

"Look out!" Penny yelled, launching herself at the bear.

"ROOOOOOAR!"

Vincent pulled his head back out of the car. His nose was full of porcupine quills.

"Make an immediate left turn," said the navigation voice.

The kids turned the wheel to the left. The truck swerved into the El Rancho Camelot Estates.

The truck headed straight for a model home. Two giant inflatable balloons — one of a knight on horseback and one of a court jester — were tied outside.

The kids saw them first.

"Oooh, power-ups!" Quillo grinned.

The kids steered the truck right for the balloons.

Vincent, clinging to the top of the truck, looked up. "Huh?" he said.

The truck slammed into the balloons, dragging Vincent off the hood and down the back of the truck. He grabbed for the back doors' handles. The doors ripped off the truck.

The balloons pulled Vincent, still holding the doors, up into the sky.

He roared furiously. *"RRRR-JJJJ!"*

In the truck, the animals cheered, forgetting about the van for a moment.

It was a moment too long.

A half block away, Gladys Sharp was desperately spraying perfume all over her house. She backed out of the door in disgust. She'd never get the place smelling right again.

RJ and the others grabbed for the wheel, but it was too late. The truck barreled at full speed into a YOUR SPEED sign, which registered ninety miles an hour as it slammed onto its side, creating a ramp.

"Bonus points!" Spike shouted gleefully, as the

truck careened up the ramp and launched itself into the air, soaring straight for Gladys's house.

Gladys turned as a shadow fell across her yard. She glanced up and stared in horror.

"Nooooooo!" she screamed as the truck flew over her head and crashed into her house.

"You have arrived," said the navigation system.

"*Awwww*. Game over," Spike said with a groan.

Inside the truck — which was now inside the house — the animals and Dwayne had been knocked silly by the impact.

Dwayne groaned. His eyes fluttered open.

There were animals everywhere.

"Yah!" he exclaimed, grabbing for them.

RJ darted out of the way. "Come on," he called to the others.

Luckily, Dwayne was still in his seat belt. He struggled to get it off as the animals escaped from the truck. They left the house through the cat door.

Then they headed for the hedge.

On the other side, they all stopped short. They stared at one another, stunned.

"Did we make it?"

"Oh, that was close."

"Alright!"

RJ looked around. "Lou? Penny? The kids here? Hammy? What are you waving at?"

Hammy looked up. "Scary clown," he said.

Everyone looked up.

Vincent was hanging from the giant balloons, which had gotten stuck in a tree right above their heads.

As the animals watched in horror, the balloon strings snapped.

Vincent dropped to the ground. He pulled a porcupine quill out of his nose and popped the balloons, one at a time. Then he glared at the animals and started towards them.

"RUN!!!!!"

The animals raced back through the hedge into Gladys's backyard again.

But Dwayne was waiting for them . . . this time armed with a cattle prod.

"Ha-ha!" he laughed.

Gladys appeared from the other side of the house, holding a weed whacker. "Filthy creatures!" she hissed.

The animals raced for the hedge and disappeared inside, hiding in the branches.

Dwayne poked the cattle prod into the hedge. It was followed by the weed whacker. The whacker's whirring blades chewed up branches and leaves, narrowly missing the terrified animals.

The animals pulled back, shaking. Then Vincent's claw swiped at them from the other side of the hedge.

The animals desperately dodged the weed whacker, the cattle prod, and Vincent's claws, racing up and down through the hedge.

Then the weed whacker made contact with Vincent's swiping paw.

Vincent roared in pain.

The cattle prod came through the hedge, hitting Vincent in the nose.

Vincent roared again. Then he balled up his paw and punched it through the hedge, hitting Dwayne in the nose. Dwayne stumbled back.

"So, you guys wanna party, do ya?" Dwayne said, recovering. "Alright then. Let's party!"

Dwayne poked the cattle prod towards Vincent. Vincent grabbed a chunk of hedge that the porcupine kids were hiding in.

Penny and Lou pulled the kids back to safety.

RJ gritted his teeth. "That's it! Verne, get everybody out of here. I'll distract him."

"Huh?" Verne turned to RJ. "Are you crazy? He'll kill you!"

"Yeah, I know," RJ said. "That's because I'm the one he wants. You take care of your family, Verne."

"I intend to," Verne said stubbornly. "The *whole* family. There's got to be something we can do."

Suddenly, Hammy started to jump up and down.

"Verne! Verne! I've got an idea!"

Hammy popped open a can of cola and started to guzzle it down.

Verne, RJ, and the others stared at him. It took them a second, but then they realized what Hammy was going to do.

While Hammy kept guzzling cola, the others kept dodging Vincent's claws and the cattle prod and weed whacker.

Then, when Hammy was ready, RJ poked his head out of the hedge and stared at Vincent.

"You know, Vincent?" he said. "You were right. They do fit perfectly on your tongue."

He popped a potato chip into his mouth.

Vincent roared in fury and launched himself at RJ.

"Now, Hammy!" Ozzie shrieked. "Go go goooooooo!"

It was Hammy Time.

Hammy had always been fast. But at that moment, he was so fast that the earth seemed to slow down to a crawl as he moved through the hedge and into Gladys's backyard. He got to the ON/OFF switch of the Depelter Turbo in record time. He flipped it on. Then he casually dodged the laser beams as they came on, one by one, while he raced back across the lawn.

In the meantime, as Vincent continued to fly towards him, RJ found himself wearing Verne's shell.

RJ smiled.

The now-naked Verne pulled the line of the pocket fisherman, which was attached to his shell, yanking RJ and the shell out of the way of the flying bear.

Vincent continued to zoom forward through the hedge and into Gladys's backyard. He crashed to the ground next to Gladys and Dwayne, passing directly through a laser beam.

Nearby, a large willow tree slowly opened, revealing the Depelter Turbo in all its evil glory. Gladys, Dwayne, and Vincent stared at it in horror.

"The Depelter Turbo," Dwayne moaned. "Prepare for a wad of stinging."

Watching from the hedge, the animals put on goggles and visors to protect their vision.

Then . . .

A huge blast of light and electricity was let loose on Gladys's backyard. Rocket launchers launched rockets. Things exploded with a huge bang.

A blast of heat swept towards the animals through the hedge, plastering back their fur.

RJ pulled out a pack of microwave popcorn and held it up in front of him.

The popcorn popped.

He offered some to Verne, who was now back in his shell.

They both munched quietly and watched in awe as Gladys' backyard was completely destroyed.

Finally, the explosions died down. A cloud of smoke drifted away.

On the other side of the hedge, Vincent, Dwayne, and Gladys were trapped in a giant cage.

The rest of the backyard was a blackened crater. Even the Depelter itself had been fried.

"Ooooh," Dwayne said. "That stung like I knew it would."

RJ and Verne looked at one another and grinned.

Hammy let out a giant burp and passed out.

An hour or so later, Vincent, strapped to a dolly, was being rolled into a police van.

Gladys was in handcuffs.

"Do you realize that was a Depeltor Turbo?" A policeman asked her. "That thing is illegal in forty-eight states."

"It was him," Gladys shouted. "He sold it to me. This had nothing to do with me!"

"It was in your yard," said another police officer. "Your name's on the contract, so you can tell it to the judge."

"No! It's not my fault! Let go of me!! I *can't* be arrested! I'm President of the Homeowner's Association!"

Gladys started struggling wildly. Both of the policemen had to grab hold of her to keep her from breaking away.

While the police subdued the flailing Gladys, Dwayne decided to take advantage of the distraction and tiptoe away. He climbed quietly over the fence, landing in the neighboring yard with a thump—and a squeak.

"Play?" Nugent barked hopefully.

Dwayne turned around slowly. A giant Rottweiler was standing there, wagging its tail.

"Oh, no," Dwayne bawled. "No, no, no, no, nooooooo!"

"Play!" Nugent barked happily.

ELEVEN

On the other side of the hedge, the animals were in an uproar of excitement.

"Jeepers!" said Penny. "We did it!"

"Good for us!" Ozzie said, clapping Lou on the back.

"Woohoo!" the porcupine kids yelled. "Gimme some! Gimme some!"

RJ gazed at everyone. He smiled slightly. Then he picked up his golf bag and turned to go.

Verne saw him starting to leave.

"Hey, RJ?" he called. "Uh, you know, just for the record, had you told us that, you know, you owed food to a bear, we would have just given it to you."

RJ turned back. "Really?"

"Yeah," said Verne. "That's what families do. They look out for each other."

RJ scratched his head. "I've never had anything like that."

Verne smiled. "Well, then, you don't know what you've been missing. This is the gateway to the good life. So . . . whaddaya say? Wanna be part of it?"

RJ dropped his bag happily.

Hammy wiped his nose with his paw. "Oh, come *here*," he sniffed.

He ran over to RJ and gave him a big hug. The others joined in.

RJ hugged them back.

"Welcome to the family!" they shouted.

The porcupine kids jumped into the group. "Awesome!" they yelled.

"Ouch!" said RJ, smiling as he pulled a quill out of his ear.

Verne stared at the happy group. He blinked back a tear. There was nothing like family.

Then his tail began to tingle.

"Hey, RJ," he said, starting to worry. "Are there any other animals that you owe anything to? Like, uh, lions or tigers, or gorillas?"

"No," RJ replied with a grin.

"Alright," Verne said, "I don't mean to grill ya, but . . ."

WIN
A 3-Pack of DVD Games!

DreamWorks
OVER THE HEDGE™

WACKY MOMENTS IN (HUMAN) HISTORY

Plus

DreamWorks
SHREK
TOTALLY TANGLED TALES™

and

DreamWorks
MADAGASCAR™
ANIMAL TRIVIA DVD GAME

b= bEQUAL
Everyone Can Play!

✂ **cut along the hedge**

OVER 50 PRIZES! TO ENTER:

Answer these three questions and register online at bequal.com/othbook

OR

Fill out this page, cut along the hedge and mail your entry to: bEQUAL / OTH Book Sweepstakes
526 Bryant St
Palo Alto, CA 94301

For hints, a list of prizes and complete sweepstakes rules, visit bequal.com/othbook.

YOUR NAME

PARENT'S NAME

PARENT'S E-MAIL

ADDRESS

CITY   STATE   ZIP

PHONE   MALE/FEMALE   AGE

1 What bright yellow symbol was worn as a pin by millions of people in the 1970s?
Unscramble the words: AMY ICES ELF

____ ____ ____

____ ____ ____

2 Is this for real? Humans can lick their own elbows. *Circle one.*

For Real!   Not For Real!

3 In the movie Over the Hedge™, what is the exterminator's first name? *Circle One.*

A) Darrell   C) Eugene

B) Dwayne   D) Ernest

Free Popcorn when you see

DREAMWORKS

OVER THE HEDGE

Opening in theatres May 19

BRUCE WILLIS · GARRY SHANDLING · STEVE CARELL · WILLIAM SHATNER · WANDA SYKES · NICK NOLTE

Taking back the neighborhood one snack at a time

DREAMWORKS
OVER THE HEDGE
From the creators of SHREK and MADAGASCAR
MAY 19

FREE SMALL POPCORN

Please bring in this book page to any of the theatres below playing DreamWorks Animation's **OVER THE HEDGE** to receive **ONE FREE SMALL POPCORN**.

CINEMARK
The Best Seat In Town

CROWN THEATRES
crowntheatres.com